Her sobs subsided into the smoke and fire scent of him and the too-human feel of his body against hers. She lifted her head and their gazes met. Her breath quickened as his eyes transformed from warm brown to blackest night. Was his head lowering, were his lips moving closer? Please, yes.

Then something beat against the window. Wings. Big wings, far too large to be a bird. Arousal transformed to alarm. "What is that?" she asked. "It's those things, isn't it?"

Raziq hesitated and then nodded.

"Are they trying to get in?"

"They know you now. That sort likes attention. They crave your fear," he added.

"Lord," she said, covering her mouth, remembering the terrible flying beings who looked like badly decomposed corpses.

"The creatures outside can't harm you. Think of them as New York pigeons."

She snorted, but couldn't suppress a smile.

"Here, get into bed. Get some rest. You've absorbed a lot of information today."

Numb, Jasmine obediently climbed under the covers and pulled them over her head. She felt Raziq move away from the bed. "Don't go," she said, reaching for him. At that moment she needed him as much as the air she breathed.

Her pulses pounded as she heard his clothes dropping to the floor and she felt the bed shifting as he crawled under the blankets. He pulled her to him and spooned his hard body against hers.

LOVE'S POTION

Monica Jackson

Dafina
Books

KENSINGTON PUBLISHING CORP.
http://www.kensingtonbooks.com

DAFINA BOOKS are published by

Kensington Publishing Corp.
850 Third Avenue
New York, NY 10022

All Kensington titles, imprints and distributed lines are
available at special quantity discounts for bulk purchases for
sales promotion, premiums, fund-raising, educational or in-
stitutional use.

Special book excerpts or customized printings can also be
created to fit specific needs. For details, write or phone the
office of the Kensington Special Sales Manager: Kensington
Publishing Corp., 850 Third Avenue, New York, NY 10022.
Attn. Special Sales Department. Phone: 1-800-221-2647.

Dafina Books and the Dafina logo Reg. U.S. Pat. & TM Off.

First Printing: September 2005
10 9 8 7 6 5 4 3 2 1

Printed in the United States of America

1

Jasmine Flynn bolted upright in bed at the scream of sirens outside her bedroom window. The sirens faded to a long, slow wail as she groped for a lamp. Apprehension flooded her as her eyes adjusted to the unfamiliar dark and sinister room.

Then the lamp's light threw the dingy off-white walls into focus, and the used dresser no longer looked like a demon crouched in the corner. Once-eerie sounds transformed to the leaky bathroom faucet drip, drip, dripping as the ancient radiator blew off steam.

Jasmine threw the blankets off, irritated and way too awake. She peered out of the frosted window. Three A.M. and the streets below still teemed with people like rush hour at high noon. New York City never rolled up the sidewalks. Unnatural, the way New York stole away her nights.

Jasmine walked across the cold tiles of the tiny studio apartment to the kitchenette and filled the teapot with water. The perfume bottle she'd left on the dresser caught her eye. She'd bought it yesterday from a junk store on her lunch break—a beautiful thing. Intricately crafted, iridescent glass threaded with gold and glossed with a patina of age. The stopper scintillated like diamond scattering color.

She'd found the bottle buried under heaps of old fabrics. The shop owner had gazed at it as if he'd never seen the bottle before. He hadn't wanted to sell it to her. But she had to make the frivolous purchase, even though with New York costs and prices, her C.P.A. salary didn't stretch as far as it had in Georgia. She insisted that he name a price. When she heard the outrageous sum, she passed over her credit card with nary a flinch.

Jasmine picked up the bottle. What old-fashioned fragrance did it hold? Its scent had probably soured. She tugged at the stopper. It didn't budge. She struggled with it a few minutes, then growled with frustration and yanked at the stopper with her teeth.

A hot wind rushed against her face. Startled, Jasmine dropped the bottle. It rolled on the carpet and a spume of a smoky substance issued from it. She clenched the hard stopper between her teeth as the smoky cloud grew bigger. Was it steam or fog? Was it toxic? What the hell had been in that bottle?

Jasmine had always known that a for-real horror film couldn't have black folk in it because as soon as the freaky stuff started, that was when any sensible brother or sister would hit the door. So why was she standing there? Jasmine panicked, too scared to scream. Instead, she croaked and fell backward on the bed.

"You better spit out that stopper in your mouth," he said, his voice deep, husky, and altogether too calm and reasonable. "You look like you're going to choke on it."

Jasmine spit out the stopper and dived for the phone.

He waved his hand. "Lady, you might as well chill. I'm not going to hurt you."

Might as well chill? Spooky man had to be kidding. She lifted the phone and frantically pushed 911, her fingers trembling. She lifted the phone to her ear. It was dead. Her stomach twisted and she stared up at him, her gaze full of dread. *Too damn scared to scream.*

He shook his head at her. "Calling 911 wasn't a good idea anyway. Do you realize they charge to come out? A good amount, too." He took a step toward her.

Jasmine finally found her voice. She let loose a screech that shook the windows. She bounded off the bed. *Feet, don't fail me now.* But to get to the door of her tiny studio apartment, she'd have to pass right by him.

He crouched next to the door with both hands clapped over his ears. "In the name of the Most High, please stop that noise," he begged. "It's worse than the Hall of Banshees."

The teakettle shrieked and he flinched. Jasmine decided she'd have to take another approach. Her hands shaking, she moved the kettle off the burner, pulled out the largest carving knife she had, and wheeled to face him.

"Get out of my house. Get out this second or I swear I'll carve you like a Thanksgiving turkey!" she yelled.

He straightened and lifted his eyebrow at the knife. "Supposing I did leave—then you wouldn't get your wish."

Jasmine tightened her hold on the knife and

wished fervently she believed in owning guns. "What wish?"

"I'm a djinni—from the bottle." He pointed to the perfume bottle on the floor. "You saw the visual effects. You opened the bottle, released me, and now you get a wish. I thought everybody knew how it worked."

Her eyes narrowed. He wore blue jeans and a white T-shirt with rolled-up sleeves. Was that a pack of Newports stuck in the shirt cuff? "A djinni?"

He sighed. "Commonly known as a genie, but I much prefer—"

"You don't look like a genie. You don't talk like a genie. Where is your genie outfit?"

He grimaced. "What do you think a djinni is supposed to look and sound like? Frankly, dressing up in Aladdin togs is not exactly my style. The whole shiny genie getup looks sort of gay, don't you think?" He gave her a disarming grin.

The finest man she'd ever seen in her life had come out of a sparkly cloud from a perfume bottle, and now he was leaning against her wall telling her that genie outfits looked gay. She pinched herself hard. This had to be a dream.

He sauntered to her kitchen and peered into her refrigerator. "Not much for cooking, are you?" he asked.

His back was exposed. Maybe she should stab him. But she heard herself saying instead, "I didn't know genies ate."

"Only when we want to. Mind if I make a sandwich?"

An intruder was asking her if she minded if he prepared food in her kitchen?

She decided to ignore him, in hopes that he'd go away. She pulled out a pair of jeans from her dresser, handily adjacent to the kitchen, and quickly pulled them on.

He washed lettuce, then spread mayonnaise on white bread. She took the opportunity to pull a sweater over her head. It looked weird over her nightgown, but the more coverage she had, the safer she felt.

He laid half a pack of bologna on the sandwich and topped it with three pieces of cheese. "Want one?" he asked.

A polite intruder. She pulled on her running shoes.

"Suit yourself. But you're kind of scrawny. You should eat." He stuck his head back into her refrigerator. "Got anything other than diet soda?"

Jasmine's nerves stretched to a thread and snapped. "No! Get out of my refrigerator and explain yourself!"

"I thought I just did. Milk will have to do, I guess." He rummaged in her cabinets until he found a large glass and filled it to the brim.

Jasmine edged to the door while he flopped his long body into her lone recliner in front of the television, set his glass down on her end table, and chomped contentedly on his sandwich. Her hand was on the doorknob when suddenly he paused mid-chew. "Got any potato chips?" he mumbled around a mouthful of sandwich.

This was not how an intruder was supposed to behave. Worse, he turned on the TV and was flipping channels with her remote. He settled on a 24-hour news channel.

"Depressing. When are you humans ever going to get it right?" he muttered to the television. "Hey, would you get me a napkin?" he called.

Jasmine handed him a stack of napkins from

her tiny kitchen table, then snapped, "When you barge into a woman's apartment, do you always make yourself a sandwich?"

"Only when she doesn't have anything better to eat. Thanks for the napkins."

He gave her a grateful grin, causing her stomach to lurch. The man looked simply too good. The whole thing had to be a dream, she decided. The intruder was her dream man. How could he be otherwise? Look at him! He was tall, at least six feet, two inches, with deep bronze skin. He wore jeans that fit his long, sexy thighs like a glove and a white T-shirt with the sleeves rolled up on his muscled biceps. His hair was cropped short with big crisp black curls. A gold hoop earring encrusted with tiny diamond and sapphire stones dangled from his left ear. His features were chiseled and so handsome, he was breathtaking. His wicked grin showed teeth so white they gleamed.

Her mind lingered on several interesting possibilities that she and Dream Man could get into.

So, she did the sensible thing. She dropped the jeans and sweater on the floor and climbed back into bed. The hell with it. As soon as Dream Man finished his snack, he could dive onto the bed with her and they'd get to the good part. All in all, this could be a very satisfying dream.

"You say you're a genie?" Jasmine asked, making conversation while she impatiently waited for him to finish his sandwich and get the party started.

"Right," he mumbled around a mouthful of sandwich.

"And I get three wishes, whatever I want?"

He took a gulp of milk. "Not three wishes, one wish."

"I thought genies always gave three wishes," Jasmine said, frowning.

"That's a myth. You get one wish. The rules are that you have to say the wish three times for it to come true. Oh, and there are stipulations."

"Stipulations?" Her dreams had never had stipulations before.

He wiped his mouth with a napkin, swung his long legs over the side of the recliner, and stood. Reaching into his pocket, he pulled out an impressive scroll that unwound to the floor.

"This is the short version," he said apologetically. "Your wish can be for personal gain only," he read. "No wishes for world peace or any other far-fetched altruism. No wishes for somebody else, unless there's a significant element of personal gain, of course. No coercion of another human, no torture, no death wishes. Wishes are covered by the following clauses—"

"What's your name? Do I call you Genie?" Jasmine interrupted. She couldn't take her eyes off him. Damn, he was fine. She'd never realized she could imagine a man who looked that luscious. But he talked too much. His fingers were long, slender and elegant. She imagined his hands on her body and her throat dried. *Less talk and more action, Dream Man.*

He hesitated. "My name is Raziq. I really should finish going over the policies and procedures."

"Sit, Rayzeek." Jasmine patted the bed next to her. "Tell me about yourself." It was way past time this dream became more interesting.

"It's Raziq," he said.

She turned on her side, letting the sheet fall away. He moved toward her.

"Can genies . . . ?" Her gaze drifted below his waist.

"Only when we want to," he said with a salacious leer to let her know without a doubt where he stood.

A man who looked like that could get away with any leer he chose to give, she thought. He touched her. His hand traced the line of her thigh. Fire. Her body burned in reponse. Her breath quickened as she felt her nipples harden against the fabric of her gown while moist heat seeped through her.

"I can grant your wish," he whispered, his voice husky, his hand moving to her panties.

Jasmine drew back, her eyes narrow. "I'd have to use a wish for you to . . . to . . . you know?"

His teeth gleamed. "I'm here to grant your one desire. And if this is what you want"—his hand moved to his belt—"I'm more than happy to comply."

"Hold up! You mean, if we did it—that would use up my wish?"

"Isn't that what I said?" he answered, unbuckling his belt.

Jasmine sighed. Even her dreams were jacked up. "That's hardly fair."

"Few things are."

His jeans dropped to the floor. His T-shirt followed. Jasmine gasped at the awesome display of male pulchritude. Cut muscles, not too bulky, without an ounce of fat on his body, all covered with delicious brown pecan skin. A redbone man— probably mixed with something. Too fine. His broad shoulders, lightly furred chest, and rippling six-pack narrowed to a perfect triangle. And then there was the bulge his briefs covered. His mighty bulge.

Lord ha' mercy. Jasmine looked around on her

bedside table for something to fan her hot cheeks. This dream might be too much for her to handle.

He fluffed the pillow next to her. Then he crawled into her bed and pulled the blankets over his head. "Wake me up when you decide what you want to do," he said, his voice muffled. He flipped over to his side and promptly started to gently snore.

Was that it? He was going to sleep? He had to be kidding. "Wake up!" She shook his shoulder. "You need to leave."

He muttered something unintelligible, not moving.

"Get up and get out! Or I will have the police come and remove you, I swear!"

He said something that sounded like a curse and stood in a fluid motion. Jasmine drew back, suddenly afraid.

But he only glowered down at her as he reached for his jeans and T-shirt. "Sheesh, lady, you won't give a guy a break, will you?"

Jasmine shrieked as he dissolved in a shower of sparks and steam and whooshed back into the bottle. The stopper flew through the air and jumped into the bottle top as if a tiny door had slammed.

Jasmine blinked once, twice. Well, well. She'd finally lost her last cookie. She'd known it was coming. The last year had been hell and she'd been expecting this nervous breakdown. She'd earned it. What is a sista supposed to do in these circumstances?

She frowned. She'd go to work as usual, call her shrink, and beg that he squeeze her in. Professional advice: that's what she needed.

Jasmine felt better as she carefully picked up the perfume bottle from the carpet, wrapped it in a layer of paper towels, and set it carefully in her purse. All things considered, if she was going to lose her mind—going off the deep end with a hunky genie of her very own wasn't half bad.

2

Dr. Takesaki leaned back in his overstuffed leather chair and surveyed Jasmine through half-lowered lids. "What's going on?"

Perched on the edge of a similar chair adjacent to him, Jasmine shifted. Dr. Takesaki had kindly worked her into his schedule over his lunch break, alarmed at her uncharacteristic fluster when she'd called him that morning. Telling him about the genie was harder than she'd thought. *Yo doc, this fine man materialized out of this perfume bottle and . . .* Yep, it was hard.

She dug in her purse, took out the perfume bottle bundled in white paper towels, and laid it on the arm of his chair.

Dr. Takesaki edged to the far side of his chair. "What is that?" he asked, giving it a look she assumed he reserved for examining the soles of his shoes after stepping in dog doo-doo on the street.

Jasmine unwrapped the paper towels from

around the bottle, and Dr. Takesaki looked relieved and settled back in the center of his chair.

She proffered him the perfume bottle. He raised an eyebrow and didn't touch it. "It's very pretty. So what's going on with you?" he repeated.

Jasmine laid the perfume bottle on the end table, leaned back in her chair, and focused on a spot in the ceiling. *Nope, not easy at all.* "Late last night. Early morning, really—um, a genie came out from that bottle."

Silence.

Jasmine cleared her throat and kept her gaze fixed on the spot. "He didn't look much like a genie. He looked like a regular guy. He wore jeans. He was very handsome, though. Gorgeous, even." Words tripped over each other in her haste to get them out. "He ate a bologna sandwich and then he took off his clothes and got into my bed—"

A strangled sound emanated from Dr. Takesaki's direction. Alarmed, Jasmine stared at him. Dr. Takesaki was looking suspiciously like he was trying not to laugh.

Her eyes narrowed.

"Do go on," Dr. Takesaki said, his voice strained. "You were at the part when he got into your bed naked."

"He kept his briefs on! Those white Fruit of the Loom kind."

Dr. Takesaki coughed. "Of course."

Jasmine shot him an indignant glance.

"Then he went to sleep," she said, still peeved.

More silence.

"Well? Aren't you going to say something?"

"Is that all?" Did Dr. Takesaki look disappointed?

"I told him to leave and he smoked back into the bottle."

"Ahhhhhh. And you felt unsatisfied? Sexually frustrated?"

"Yes. No! I think you're missing the point, Dr. Takesaki. I *saw* a genie come out of that bottle." She pointed. "I'm afraid I'm losing my mind!"

"Because of your unsatisfied desires?"

"No!" She restrained herself from yelling at Dr. Takesaki, although she really, really wanted to. "Because. I. Saw. A. Genie. Come. Out. Of. That. Damned. Perfume bottle!" She couldn't prevent her voice from going up. "Do you get it now?"

"Could this handsome male genie merely be a reflection of your unsatisfied sexual desires?" Dr. Takesaki mused.

No, she wouldn't hit the man. Knocking him upside the head wouldn't be appropriate at all. But how else could she budge Dr. Takesaki's sexual obsession? She'd heard that was an occupational hazard of being a shrink, but still.

"I think the genie was a reflection of what came out of that perfume bottle," Jasmine said, her voice dry.

"Did he want to satisfy your every desire?"

"Yes. I mean no! He would only give me one wish."

"Only one?"

"And he told me if we made love, that would use up my wish."

"That's quite interesting." Obviously Dr. Takesaki must have felt as if he had made quite an understatement because he looked as if he was using much effort to hold back an urge to rub his hands together in glee. "You have the ultimate tool of satisfaction at your disposal, yet he denies you. How do you feel about that?"

"He had some nerve . . . Hey! You keep missing

the point. I'm seeing imaginary—DON'T DO THAT!"

Dr. Takesaki had pulled out the bottle stopper and was sniffing the opening.

"No fragrance," he said, handing the bottle back to her. "Sorry. But why did you give this to me if you didn't want me touch it?"

"I'm afraid he'll come out," she said, stuffing the stopper back into the bottle.

"I doubt it," Dr. Takesaki said.

Jasmine frowned. "Why do you suppose that?"

"Because we both know that genie is mostly here." He tapped his head.

"You may know it. But I'm not so sure, Doc. That's why I'm here."

Dr. Takesaki grinned. "A breakthrough. Your feelings of betrayal from your married ex-lover are finally dissipating to let your sexual desires through! You thought you had him, yet he denies you. So much like Keith!"

Good Lord, what had Dr. Takesaki been smoking? "The genie has nothing to do with Keith."

"Ahhhh," he said.

Before she gave in to her impulse to slap the cheerful, smug look off her doctor's face, she pulled out the stopper and called out, "Raziq, come forth."

Dr. Takesaki shifted uncomfortably in his chair. "I don't recommend that you unleash your sexual desires here and now. Perhaps—"

"Shush. Raziq?" she called.

Nothing. She peered into the bottle. Empty. She sniffed it. No smell. She turned it upside down and shook it. Nothing. It figured.

"You're not crazy," Dr. Takesaki said. "You have

been hurt recently. Badly hurt. The mind has all sorts of tricks to protect and educate itself in a way the conscious mind can accept. Go with the flow, Jasmine. Enjoy your genie."

"But he was so real," she whispered.

"This is a breakthrough," Dr. Takesaki said again. "We'll talk about it next session, okay?"

It was a dismissal. Poor Dr. Takesaki was probably starving.

Jasmine stood. "Thanks for seeing me. You really don't think I'm crazy?"

He shook his head. "No, you're not crazy," he said with a kind smile.

She exhaled. "Good."

"You tell me what happens between you and the genie next time, okay? Maybe he will change his mind about the lovemaking?"

Jasmine glowered at him. "Good-bye, Dr. Takesaki."

Jasmine picked up Chinese on the way home. She should have gone to the gym, but she didn't feel up to facing the after-work crowd's jockeying to get one of the coveted cardio machines. Last time she went to the gym, she thought a fight was going to break out by the treadmills. By February, the crowd would thin, their New Year's resolve faded. Until then, it was nearly impossible to muster up the fortitude to face the gym, although she sorely missed her workouts.

She let herself into her tiny apartment. Kicking off her shoes, she changed to sweats, neatly hanging her navy blue suit in the closet. She turned on the evening news and settled in her recliner with a carton of shrimp lo mein, ready to dig into her lonely evening. She eyed her purse sitting on the end table.

With a sigh, she retrieved the perfume bottle and twisted off the stopper. She sniffed the empty bottle. It must have been a dream after all, she thought. It was almost disappointing because, damn, that genie was—suddenly, Jasmine yelped as what felt like a warm, moist wind went up her nose. She sneezed violently.

"God bless you," a husky masculine voice said near her ear.

Jasmine jumped and knocked the ice-cold can of diet Coke into her lap. She cursed as she leapt out of the chair.

"Girl, you could make a sailor blush," he said.

She glared at him as she grabbed a pair of jeans from her dresser drawer and went to the bathroom to remove her sweatpants. She sure wasn't dreaming now. A freaking genie was standing in the middle of her studio.

Jasmine stepped tentatively out of the bathroom.

Raziq was stretched out in her recliner chowing down on her Chinese food, wearing blue jeans and a white T-shirt.

"I dried the chair," he said, brandishing his chopsticks. "Do you have anything to drink besides diet—"

"Get out of my chair! And how dare you eat my dinner?" Jasmine roared.

He lifted his brow at her. "Since you put it like that . . ." He moved out of the chair with one graceful movement. "Sorry about your food. I always seem to be starving when I leave that bottle. . . ."

He grinned at her. "Tell you what, I'll take you out to eat to make it up."

Jasmine's mouth snapped shut on her retort. *Go with the flow,* she heard Dr. Takesaki's voice say. "Why didn't you come out when I opened the bottle in Dr. Takesaki's office?" she asked.

"I don't put on a horse-and-pony show for just anybody. Djinn Statute 1.278 states that thou shalt not reveal yourself to mortals without due cause."

"You revealed quite a bit of yourself to me," she said, remembering smooth copper skin and cut muscle.

"You opened the bottle, lady. That's how it works. Your wish is my command." He made a slight wave of his arm, and a pair of pristine white Nikes appeared in his hands. He sat on the bed to don his shoes. "Where do you think we should eat?" he asked.

Jasmine blinked. It all seemed so normal. But a genie was sitting on her bed and pulling on magically appearing expensive white sneakers over sparkling clean white cotton socks and wondering where they should eat.

"Italian might be good."

"Yeah, I like that," he said. "That Dr. Takesaki thinks you're hot, you know," he said.

"Thinks I'm hot?" Her face heated as she thought of plump, balding, and gentle Dr. Takesaki. "He's my psychiatrist. He doesn't think I'm hot."

"He's a man. How can he not? You are like a honey-colored cat, sleek and beautiful with big eyes and graceful ferocity."

His voice was soft and husky and sent a shiver down her spine right to . . . ? "Stop it. You're being ridiculous. It would be unethical for—and Dr. Takesaki is very ethical."

"There are no ethics that can police a man's

thoughts about a woman." He stood, his shoes laced. "Shall we go?"

A thought struck her. "Will this use up my wish?"

"No. You get a free ride for dinner." Wicked glints shone from his eyes as his gaze floated over her body.

Images of the sort of ride he could choose to give her filled her mind, and she almost choked.

"We can talk over food. Come," he said, his hand on the door.

"I need to change first."

"You look fine."

"Impatient for a genie, aren't you?" Jasmine said. "Hold up a sec." She pulled off the scrunchie pulling back her hair after she'd loosed it from its tight and confining businesslike French roll, and it cascaded past her shoulders, a wavy black cloud. "How long were you a genie in that bottle?" she asked.

"Djinni, not genie. I was last released from the bottle in 1969."

Jasmine drew a sharp breath. "1969! How do you know what's happening now so well? You seem like a regular guy."

"I can hear what goes on outside the bottle. Besides, I get television."

"Inside a perfume bottle?"

"Sure. Satellite and all the premium cable stations, and movies too. I like HBO."

Jasmine's temples started throbbing with tension. A TV-watching, movie-loving genie. It was too much. She turned to her dresser and picked up a hairpin to put her hair up again.

Raziq touched her hand. His touch burned.

"Let your hair be," he said, standing far too close. "I prefer it like that."

Heat flushed through Jasmine in a wave, causing her to lose every bit of her hard-won composure. She drew in a sharp breath. He smelled of sandalwood and fire. Jasmine moistened her lips with her tongue as arousal warred for space within her already-stirred emotions. *What was happening to her?*

3

The restaurant was a small, family-owned place, known for the food. Dark and intimate, it was made for lovers.

Jasmine ordered lasagna while Raziq ordered a double portion of vegetable penne with extra olive oil and a bottle of good rosé.

"What do you think you're going to wish for?" Raziq asked, munching on a breadstick. The waiter returned with the wine, giving her a moment's reprieve.

The wish. She had never really thought about it, mostly because she never really believed that he could grant a real wish. But what if he could?

"I'm not sure," she said.

"Most wish for wealth or success," he said.

"Do you think such wishes are best?" she asked.

"No," he said shortly.

"Why not? Wealth and success sound pretty good to me."

"Humans invariably find that neither brings them the happiness they sought. They discover that the obstacles to their happiness are as big as they ever were, only the obstacles are different."

"Then why not wish for happiness directly?"

"The problem with that wish is that only the dead have no troubles."

Jasmine's eyebrows shot up. The dead, huh? Well, that nixed that idea.

"What would you wish for?" she asked him.

Raziq looked surprised. "Nobody has ever asked me that question."

He took a sip of water. "The thing I would choose to wish for isn't possible for me to have."

"I thought magic could make anything possible."

"Not everything. It can't turn back time." He drew in a breath. "We need to concentrate on your wish."

The waiter brought a basket of steaming bread.

"Smells heavenly," Jasmine said, reaching for the butter knife.

"You need to word your wish very carefully," Raziq said. "The djinn are obligated to be very literal in wish fulfillment. Often, people find the very thing they hoped for most has transformed into a curse."

"You would do that to me?" she asked. There was something about Raziq that soothed. She'd bet money that he was *good*. Funny, she never thought of people that way—good or evil—but she supposed Raziq didn't count because he wasn't exactly a person.

"How your wish is granted isn't within my control," he said. "Wish granting is more of a group endeavor, and uses the power of every djinni in existence. It strictly follows our statutes and is thoroughly literal."

"Oh." Jasmine savored the bread and chased it with a swallow of wine.

"What are your deepest desires, your passions? These are often rooted in your experiences." His voice was low and husky.

She remembered how he had looked at her when he touched her hand, then her hair. Her thoughts melted into a jumble. He confused her, made it hard for her to think clearly, to breathe evenly. It made no sense. Nothing made any sense.

She mentally shook her head to clear it. Okay, so she wouldn't mind a tumble heels over head with this fine genie, but even the best bonin' in the world wasn't worth a wish that could grant any desire. Men who looked as good as he did never lived up to their advance billing.

"You need to wish soon," he said.

Jasmine bit her lip. Having a wish should be good enough for any woman. If wishes were fishes, everybody would be trying to drown. "You're in a hurry to get back into that bottle?" she asked.

He took a swallow of wine and looked away. "Your doctor said you'd been betrayed. Maybe you could wish for revenge or reconciliation?"

"Keith isn't worth a wish. And doesn't revenge always come back to bite you in the ass?"

"That's usually the rule. But a djinni wish would circumvent the karma," he said. "Killing him or extreme physical torture is prohibited. But impotency is a popular revenge wish," he added with a wicked grin.

"As tempting as that would be, there is no way I'm going to waste a wish on Keith."

He beamed at her. "There was pain in your voice when you first mentioned his name. Whether a

woman has the capacity to move on says something about her character."

"You care about my character?" Jasmine asked,
nonplussed. She blinked and moved the subject
back to more comfortable ground. "When I think
about getting whatever I really want—my mind
draws a blank."

"You already have all you desire in life?" Raziq
asked.

Jasmine snorted. "Please. I hate this city, hate
my job, hate—" She snapped her mouth shut before she uttered the words.

"Hate your life?" he finished for her.

Jasmine looked away, pained. "I've only been in
New York for about a month," she said slowly. "I
moved here from Macon, Georgia. I work at a
large accounting firm."

"You relocated for the job?"

"I got the job after I arrived. I'm a CPA and
employment ops have never been a big problem if
I'm not too picky."

"But your phone doesn't ring. You've spoken to
no one except your psychiatrist of anything but
work-related issues. You come straight home from
work, eat your take-out food and watch television
or read until bed. You have no lover."

Raziq's words felt like an indictment. She knew
her face reflected how she felt inside—exposed
and vulnerable—and for a moment she resented
him for it. She had more than enough reasons for
her . . . dissatisfaction.

"Why did you come here?" he asked.

She waited until the waiter set their plates in
front of them and left before answering. "I was
running away."

Raziq said nothing. She sensed he was waiting for her to continue.

"I slept with a married man for five years," she said. "He was my boss and the reason I moved to Macon from Atlanta. He asked me to be patient, wait until his children were older. So I waited . . . year after year. I wanted my own family, sure, but I wanted one with the man I thought I loved."

The fact that the pain was still so sharp surprised her. Keith wasn't worth hurting over, and she wondered why the pain didn't fade.

"Go on," Raziq said.

"Keith told me that he'd left his wife," she continued. "He said he wanted to live before he got too old to enjoy life. I was ecstatic. I knew that with his marriage finally out of the way, he'd openly declare his love for me and we could marry and start our own family. After all, that's what I'd been waiting for all those years. But, but . . . ," she said, dropping her head.

"It's a classic story," Raziq said. "There's no need to tell me the ending if it pains you."

"I need to finish. Apparently Keith's idea of living didn't include me. He confessed our affair to his ex-wife. She confronted me with every little detail, every lie I'd told to sneak away with Keith. From her lips, what I believed was the pure, self-sacrificing love we shared seemed sordid and dirty. I was a fool and no better woman." Jasmine shook her head.

"Keith packed up and moved to Atlanta. He didn't say a word. No hello, good-bye, or kiss my ass. I found out where he was and called him. He told me to leave him the hell alone and hung up on me." Tears stung her eyes at the memory. "I was a fool."

"Maybe. But he was the one who made the vows. He had his cake, overate it, and thought he could vomit out the consequences. He betrayed his family, and accepted your love, then trampled on it. He did the greater evil."

"And I only the lesser? So, now he's living it up in Atlanta and look at me."

Raziq touched her hand. That curious heat burned her again. "Remember karma. It does exist, cause and effect. Look at what you have now, a wish to make true. Forgiveness exists, if you want it."

She smiled at him and toyed with her food. It was too easy to expose her soul to this man. Who was he? What was he?

"They say you can't run from yourself. Guess they're right. My mistakes follow me wherever I go."

"Look at me," Raziq commanded. She raised her gaze to his and wanted to drown in his eyes. Familiar heat rose within her. She moistened her lips.

"If you hadn't moved to New York, you never would have met me," he said.

The wish be damned, she thought, and pondered the joys of uncomplicated sex with the best-looking man she had ever seen in her life. She swallowed hard.

"Jasmine!" Jasmine looked up to see Sharon Drumm, a woman who shared an adjacent cubicle at work, bearing down on her.

"Uh, hello," Jasmine said. Sharon looked expectantly at Raziq as soon as she reached their table.

"Sharon, this is my friend, Raziq . . . ?" Jasmine said, at a loss for a last name.

"Sharon Drumm," she said, offering her hand. "I'm pleased to meet you, Raziq. I didn't quite catch your last name."

"Just Raziq," he said with his easy grin.

"Where have you been hiding this wonderful man, Jasmine?"

"In my purse," Jasmine said truthfully.

"Funny girl," Sharon said. She dropped a card on the table.

"Here's my number. Why don't you give me a call sometime?" She directed the words toward Jasmine, but her gaze didn't move from Raziq's masculine form. She flashed a smile at him and glided away.

Jasmine sucked her teeth. Did that heifer just try to cop her man from right under her nose? *Oh, no, she didn't.*

"That woman barely says hello, goodbye, or kiss my butt in the office," she said, picking up the card and tearing it in half with a flourish. "What a difference a man makes."

"Djinni" he said.

"What?"

"I'm not a man; I'm one of the djinn, and you'd do well to think on your wish." He looked around him, uncomfortable. "I'm sensing you don't have much time."

"Why the rush?"

He leaned back in his chair. "That's not it. It has to do with me. I dare not tarry long."

What the hell was he talking about? As far as she was concerned, she'd like him to tarry as long as possible.

"If you don't wish soon, you may have some . . . uncomfortable experiences," he said.

"What do you mean, uncomfortable experiences?" Was he threatening her?

"I'm nonhuman, a material magical being. Since I'm continually revealing myself to you, if you don't make your wish soon, you might see things now hidden from your eyes. Also, things that threaten me may affect you. Not good."

"What are you talking about?" Jasmine said irritably.

"There are many things in this world that you'd prefer not to know about."

"Witches, wizards, leprechauns, and the like, I suppose."

He shook his head. "Wizards and witches are human. Leprechauns are magical beings, true, but merely Irish gnomes. There are very few magical beings such as myself left in the world—the djinn, unicorns, nymphs, dragons, gnomes, trolls, and fairies. What I'm speaking of is more in the line of spirits."

"Spirits?" Jasmine laid down her fork.

"Lingering dead, elementals, occasional angels." He lifted his glass. "But you'll find the demons most alarming."

Speechless, Jasmine stared at him. All the spooky stories she had heard growing up, and everything she'd ever heard about demons ran through her mind. A lump of fear formed in her throat. Jasmine decided that he was trying to scare her. Her fear transformed to anger instantly and she felt herself tremble inside, her body heated and shook with rage.

"What sort of game are you playing?" she asked him.

He raised an eyebrow. His sardonic good looks pissed her off even more. It was crazy; he was crazy.

"I don't know how you manage the David Copperfield magic tricks, appearing and disappearing in a big puff of smoke, but now that you're talking about demons, I think it's time your game ended." Her voice was shaky and she pushed back from the table and stood.

The idea of demons rattled her. She didn't make it to church much any more, but her religious roots were deep. Her family had been fundamental Holiness folk and they had no truck with demons.

She pulled her purse strap over her shoulder. "Never mind, don't tell me about your game. I'm not that interested. Thanks for the meal, but if I ever see you again, you'll be telling the cops about your demons."

With those words, Jasmine dashed out of the restaurant. The cold air hit her as she whistled for a taxi. One pulled over to the curb immediately.

"Take me to North 113th, off Broadway," she said.

"Okay, lady." The taxi driver put the car into gear and glanced over his shoulder. Jasmine's mouth dropped open, and the contents of her stomach rose to her throat. The swarthy driver had no eyes but great gaping pits where his eyes should be. Black holes. A smell wafted from him, putrid and rotten. Sulfur? Red fires flickered in the awful emptiness of his eye sockets.

Holy Heavenly Father, it knew. She gasped, it knew she could see what it was. It reached for her. Jasmine shrieked and scrambled out of the moving taxi, falling in the street. Cars honked and tires screeched, but she didn't care; she had to get away from that thing.

She rolled on the street, her knees cracking against the pavement, and asphalt tearing at her skin, but she was so scared the pain barely registered. She jumped up, running before her feet hit the ground, heading for the sidewalk, weaving through the traffic. Her body protested the exertion with every breath. She paused at a subway station, but hesitated before going downstairs. She couldn't go . . . underneath.

She heard wings flapping—a leathery sound from above. She looked up and apparitions with skeletal faces stared down at her. Black bat wings stretched from the backs of their ugly skeletons, flesh dripping from the bones. They circled above her, laughing like hyenas.

She went down the stairs at a dead run. The turnstile stopped her and she dug in her purse for a token. She found one and dropped it in. She would not panic. No, no, no. She was only having a little psychotic break. She wouldn't make it worse by acting a fool. She didn't want to be carted off to Bellevue in a straitjacket. Not her style at all. There were medications. Medications that would make it all go away. She'd be okay. Okay.

She stood with the crowd in front of the train tracks trying not to visibly tremble. She would get on a subway and go home. Everything would be all right. Suddenly, a low voice whispered behind her and the scent of sulfur hung thick in the air. She would not look up or look around. She'd look at her feet. Feet only. But around her feet, shadows were reflected that couldn't possibly be human.

She mumbled Bible verses under her breath. People stood around her in attitudes of boredom or preoccupation. Nobody else looked around in fear and wonder. Nobody else screamed and ran. Only she heard. Only she saw.

The train pulled up and she got on, concentrating on putting one step in front of another.

When she reached her stop, Jasmine hurried up the stairs into the night. She'd make it to her apartment, as long as she didn't look up.

The sounds of leathery wings met her as she emerged from the subway station, along with mocking laughter.

Oh, shit. Demons, freaking demons. She couldn't believe it. Even though she hoped she was crazy, she probably wasn't. Raziq had warned her, and all she had done was lose her temper.

Raw and urgent fear pounded through her. Her steps speeded up to a run. When she reached her apartment building, she felt the wind from their wings as she frantically fumbled for her keys, praying to the Lord for deliverance.

Tension drained from her body when she finally slammed her apartment door behind her. She locked all four of her deadbolts securely and put on the chains. Spying the upright perfume bottle with its stopper securely in place, she drew in a relieved breath. When they'd left, the bottle had been uncapped on her kitchen table, lying on its side, the stopper about four inches away. He was back. She removed the stopper with trembling hands. Warm smoke streamed and Raziq stood in front of her, his arms folded across his chest.

"Now do you believe me?" he asked.

4

Jasmine sank to the edge of the bed and buried her face in her hands. She shuddered. She felt Raziq sitting beside her and lifted her head.

"Those were demons?"

"If they were ugly and scared you, they were."

"The taxi driver had no eyes. Demons drive taxis?" She wasn't a bit surprised.

"Only when they've possessed a human."

"Jesus," she said, and she didn't mean it as an oath, rather as a prayer. "So demons do go around possessing people and it's mere luck that I'm not spewing out pea soup while I fly toward the ceiling?"

"No, it's not luck. You generally have to make a doorway to be possessed or oppressed."

"A doorway?"

"An invitation for them to enter. And make sure you don't go playing around with a Ouija board."

"So demons don't bother you without an invite?" Jasmine exhaled with relief.

"Basically. But there are many ways of inviting evil."

She faced Raziq. "Are you evil?" she asked. Had she already let evil into her life?

"Not particularly. I have free will like a human. But, like most humans, most djinn don't willfully choose to practice evil and I certainly don't."

That was a relief. "Can those flying things outside hurt me?"

"Your body is material and they are spirit. Spirits can't directly affect the material things of the world. They can affect only your spirit and only if you allow them to do so."

"You're telling me that those things have always been present, but I just couldn't see them?"

"That's right. Frankly, you haven't seen much yet."

She buried her head in her hands. "Why? Oh, Lawd, why?"

Raziq's eyes widened at her wail, but it made her feel better. Her mother used to say that. Worked like a charm.

"Their desire is to create evil in this world," Raziq said slowly, apparently deciding to take her words literally. "There are other spirit beings who want to create good. The balance tips to one side, then the other. Right now, there's much evil."

"I get to see all this until I—"

"Make your wish and I depart. Then you'll no longer be able to perceive the unseen world."

"Not seeing something doesn't make it go away." She looked toward her window; the blinds were tightly closed. "If there's something out there, I prefer to see what it is."

Raziq covered her hand with his own. "No, you don't."

Fire. He withdrew his hand. "I'm sorry," he said.

"Sorry for what? You didn't create the demons, did you?"

He paused. "I'm sorry for touching you."

Oh. Too bad, because she wished he'd touch more of her.

"That's all right." What an understatement. She sighed. "I'm going to take a bath," she said.

"That's a good idea. You can think about your wish. You need to make it quickly."

Jasmine sank into the bathwater until bubbles tickled the tip of her nose. She sneezed. *Demons, ghosts, and monsters, oh my,* ran through her mind, a despairing refrain in her brain.

Should she wish for riches? She could get away from the necessity of being tied to an accounting job, leave New York, and build a new life. Hopefully a good one.

A good life was what she really wanted. Money was simply a means to that end. How exactly did she define a good life? What did she want? Closing her eyes, she willed herself to imagine.

She walked out on the porch wearing a soft woolen sweater and jeans. The country air was fresh and crisp, the woods piney, and the ground red clay. She was back in Georgia. Children's laughter echoed through the sunshine and bounced off crisp blue skies. Out back she heard the ax playing a steady rhythm as her man split logs for their fireplace and wood stove. Her man—loving, kind, and sexy as hell. He looked exactly like Raziq. . . .

She sat up in the tub so fast, soap bubbles got in her eyes. Was that what she wanted? Bucolic Georgia countryside, a bunch of kids, and a fine man? She wasn't the domestic type! Heavens, she'd have to learn to cook!

She thought of herself as a city girl all the way through, sassy and independent. She couldn't see herself with a rural lifestyle and a bunch of kids. But then, she'd believed that the excitement of New York City would fit her perfectly. She'd been very wrong. New York fit as well as a shoe two sizes too small.

Was a man her greatest desire? Did she crave love above all? She was lonely, true. But the thought of trusting a man with her heart again made her feel nauseous. She couldn't do it. Right now, the best thing a man could do for her, she could also get from a good vibrator. Or Raziq.

That man, genie, or whatever he was, drove her crazy. He crawled under her skin, too attractive, too nice, too much of everything to be real.

What about health and long life? But what was the point of wishing for a long life when you had to die at the end anyway? And living forever was too terrible to contemplate.

She had never desired the tiniest bit of celebrity; she'd way rather be rich than famous. As far as her looks, she was satisfied enough with hers.

In her heart, she realized that there was one thing she desired above all. She wanted her family back. She wanted them to be alive and well. She missed them so.

The night Jasmine had lost her family, she was fifteen and hanging out at her best friend Carmel's house. She was supposed to be bowling with her family, but with teenage rebellion, that night she'd refused to go.

"I'm not going to fight with you, Jas," her mother said. "But one day you'll regret the time you didn't spend with us. Every moment in your life only comes around once."

Mama had been right. The police came to her friend's door that evening and asked for her. Then they told her that her parents and younger brother had been killed in an automobile accident. Wrong place, wrong time. They'd happened across a drunk driver, multiple convictions, no license. A high speed head-on collision. Dead, all dead.

She didn't remember what happened afterward. She didn't remember anything much for a long time after that except how much she wished she were dead too, like she was supposed to be.

They locked her up in a hospital for the longest time to make sure that didn't happen.

After so many years, the memories still caused tears to rise in her eyes. Yes, if she only had one wish in the world, it would be to have her family back.

"You okay in there?" Raziq called through the door.

"I—I'm fine." She pulled the plug and let the water drain away. She felt better now that she knew what she was going to wish for—and the damned demons would be gone! *But so would the finest male you've ever met in your life.*

She toweled dry and donned a thick white terry cloth robe before venturing out into her one-room studio. Raziq was in her recliner glued to ESPN and chomping on potato chips. The scene appeared too normal for him to be a genie and her a confused woman who'd merely bought an antique perfume bottle.

"Raziq?" He looked up at her.

"I've decided on my wish."

He smiled at her and clicked the remote to turn the television off. "Good. Your wish is my command."

"Um, I wish for my family back. My nuclear family," she hurried to add as he began to frown. "My parents and my brother—that's what I want."

Raziq moved the chair upright and shook his head.

"What do you mean, no?" she said. "You said my wish was your command. C'mon, bring them back. Right here is fine." Jasmine sat on the edge of her bed and pointed to the carpet in front of her.

"It's not within my power," he said. "I can't bring back souls. Your family is long gone from this world, Jasmine."

Tears spilled from her eyes and ran down her cheeks. "What good are you, then?" she asked, her voice strangled.

He moved beside her and took her into his arms. His arms were warm and tight, holding her close. A feeling she'd never known before welled up. Comfort, safety, security—and something within broke. One of the defensive walls she carried inside crumbled and grief racked her body with sobs.

"I'm sorry," he whispered in her ear. "I would give you back your family if I could."

Her sobs subsided into the smoke scent of him and the too-human feel of his body against hers. She lifted her head and their gazes met. Her breath quickened as his eyes transformed from warm brown to blackest night. Was his head lowering, were his lips moving closer? Please, yes.

Then something beat against the window. Wings. Big wings, far too large to be a bird. Arousal transformed to alarm. "What is that?" she asked. "It's those things, isn't it?"

Raziq hesitated and then nodded.

"Are they trying to get in?"

"They know you now. That sort likes attention. They crave your fear," he added.

"Lord," she said, covering her mouth, remembering the terrible flying beings who looked like badly decomposed corpses.

"The creatures outside can't harm you. Think of them as New York pigeons."

She snorted, but couldn't suppress a smile.

"Here, get into bed. Get some rest. You've absorbed a lot of information today."

Numb, Jasmine obediently climbed under the covers and pulled them over her head. She felt Raziq move away from the bed. "Don't go," she said, reaching for him. At that moment she needed him as much as the air she breathed.

Her pulses pounded as she heard his clothes dropping to the floor and she felt the bed shifting as he crawled under the blankets. He pulled her to him and spooned his hard body against hers.

Jasmine wondered how could he not be human, not pulsing with blood as red and hot as her own? She wanted this man so badly.

"Wanting a man always has disastrous consequences," she murmured.

"Why do you say that?" Raziq asked.

She bit her lip. She hadn't really meant to express her fear out loud.

"Wanting is the natural way between a man and a woman. The consequences are also natural." He sounded worried.

Maybe it was time. He should find out how screwed up she really was before she sank deeper into this feeling. This feeling of wanting was so sharp, she couldn't tell it from need. A wanting that was deeper than sex or arousal, wanting that mere thrusting and climax couldn't assuage. She wanted his regard, his love, his fidelity . . . his soul.

She wanted him, and it terrified her more than the demons outside. "I have a poor track record with men," she said. "I'm always the one who ends up hurting and rejected." There, she said it. She'd broken one of the cardinal rules far too soon. She exposed weakness, vulnerability and a lack of self-regard. She braced herself inside for his palpable disappointment, distain and distancing. A man respected a strong woman and rejected a weak one.

"Your past track record has nothing to do with me," he said, his voice quiet. She picked up no condemnation or criticism.

"Your past affects you and you alone," he continued. "There's no need for it to spill over into our relationship, unless you choose to put it there."

His words rumbled into her ear, his mouth so close. And suddenly a pang of inner anguish knotted into frustration, her hands clenching against his chest. "My past is me," she said. "You can't possibly understand my loss."

"I think I can. I loved Hyeth, my wife, and my children. I was helpless to save them when the waters ripped them away from me."

There was such pain in his voice she raised her head, her own pain momentarily forgotten. "Raziq, I'm sorry."

"There's nothing for you to be sorry about. It happened a long time ago. The pain is only there when I choose to remember it. It's best to live in the present, most of the time, at least. In the present, the past doesn't exist."

She felt his lips, warm and firm against her temple. She closed her eyes, feeling the hard warmth of his body against hers.

"Go to sleep," he said softly.

She didn't think it would be possible, with arousal fighting the fatigue coursing through her veins. But he held her tight and she became conscious of her breath moving in and out. *Right now.* She didn't know if he said it or if it was her own thought. Jasmine drifted on her breath to a soft, cottony darkness that welcomed and soothed.

5

Jasmine opened her eyes to pale dawn seeping through the window blinds. Raziq snuggled behind her, his strong arm curved over her belly. His breathing was deep and regular and she smelled his subtle masculine scent. Smoke and fire.

She pressed her buttocks against his hard body. Right now, there wasn't a thing she wanted more than his touch. He drew in a sharp breath and his arm tightened, pulling her closer. She felt his thick length against her buttocks. Matching heat rose insistent within her, and she turned around to face him. He looked into her eyes and she sensed his rising passion, his eyes darkened as if a storm played behind them.

But he made no move toward her.

"Why not?" she asked simply, knowing he would read the meaning around the words. *Why won't you make love to me?*

"I can't. The statutes say—"

"Statutes! I can't believe you're going to quote

rules at me about sex. If you don't want me, you should at least be man enough to say it."

The taunt 'man enough' would generally enrage any man. But Raziq only looked sad. "Mating between magical beings and humans has been forbidden for thousands of years."

"Who forbids it?"

"The One who provides order for all things. Millennia ago, the hybrid children that issued from those forbidden joinings banded together and almost destroyed the human race entirely."

"But you said I could wish for it."

His face brightened. "Is that your wish?"

"No! But if I can wish for you to make love to me, how can it be forbidden?"

"The wish would override the statute preventing it. Collective magic could then ensure that there would be no pregnancy. Otherwise I can't, literally. Mating with a human, no matter how much I wanted to, would cause intense pain."

"Are you telling me it would hurt me?"

"Yes, it would hurt us both, perhaps kill us."

"I don't believe you. There's no need to lie to me because—"

Raziq pulled her into his arms so quickly that she gasped and caught her mouth with his own.

She met his passion with her own, hunger rocking her, a burning ache between her legs. Her hips rotated of their own volition seeking, seeking . . . His lips were firm and wholly masculine. Warm and human but tasting of smoke. Hot, moist warmth flooded her and an inferno rose between them as their tongues parried each other's and their bodies started to strain together. Fire.

Suddenly, Jasmine exclaimed in pain and drew back. Her mouth was on fire, literally burning. She touched her lips. "What was that?" she whispered. Her mouth felt as if it was seared. Her entire body was sore where she'd been pressed against him. What had happened to her?

Raziq threw the covers back and stood, his hand massaging his own cheek. "That's what happens between human and djinni. Passion literally ignites and we both burn." Raziq drew in a harsh breath.

His arousal was obvious at her eye level. Obvious, huge, and luscious. Jasmine drew in a shaky breath.

"I find you beautiful," he said. "There is something fascinating about you, far more than I've found in other human women. When I first sensed you, I thought you might be one of the few half-breed djinn left in the world. You excite me and I want to please you for no good reason."

"But that's not enough?" she asked.

"No, it's not enough. I'd cripple myself with pain and possibly sacrifice your life."

Jasmine was silent, considering his statement. "You know that from firsthand experience," she said, more of a statement than a question. His voice had been laced with painful memories.

Raziq got out of bed and gathered his clothes. "Unfortunately, I do," he said right before he dissipated into a plume of smoke that disappeared into the perfume bottle.

Jasmine sucked in a breath. She touched her lips, remembering the fire of his kiss, the blaze of his body. If anything might be worth dying for . . . no. It made no sense. She needed to pull herself together. She was going to be late for work if she didn't get a move on.

Twenty minutes later, her purse slung over her shoulder, Jasmine stood stock-still with her hand on her doorknob. Grotesque images flashed through her mind. Demons awaited her outside. Demons that recognized her, that reached out with skeletal, scaly hands.

Nope, she wasn't going anywhere but back to bed. Her briefcase dropped to the floor as she reached for the phone to call in sick. The flu was going around, so she might as well have it.

Her boss sounded irritated and skeptical. This was the first time she'd ever called in sick and Jasmine barely restrained herself from telling him what he could do with his job. But the rent on her crappy New York studio was astronomical. She barely kept ahead of her living expenses, and without a job, what would she do? *Go back home to Atlanta,* a treacherous thought whispered.

Go back home defeated, to looks of pity and whispers behind hands. Go back home to face all her mistakes in the flesh? No. Not an option. She'd deal with sleepless nights and the continual roar of garbage trucks. She'd battle the cockroaches and wrestle her loneliness.

She hung her suit back up in the closet and crawled into an oversize T-shirt and ratty sweatpants. Turning the television toward the bed, she tunneled under the covers, remote in hand.

She turned the television up loud so she couldn't hear anything beating or scratching against the thin glass of her windowpanes.

Jasmine stared at the perfume bottle sparkling on the bedside table, although the room was dim, with blinds closed and curtains drawn. Raziq's presence threw her loneliness into bleak relief. She picked up the bottle and held so tight that her palm grew sweaty.

She needed to make the wish. She could wish

away demons in more ways than one. Money would be a simple choice, but wishing for money felt like a waste. Maybe it was her religious background. "Money is the root of all evil," Mama said. "I don't ever want you to put money first. There's so much more to life."

Good thing Mama believed that because they sure didn't have much money. But they'd been a happy family most times. Daddy worked the night shift at the electric company. Mama stayed at home, baking, cleaning, and doing crafty stuff. A pang went through Jasmine as she realized that Mama had died at the same age she was now.

From a teenager's viewpoint, Mama seemed old and wise, but she'd been a young woman in her midthirties when she'd died. Jasmine's life was career oriented, with plenty of men, and not a domestic bone in her body. How could mother and daughter be so different?

There was another difference between them. Mama had been happy, full of joy most the time. She couldn't imagine her mother being lonely— her life was filled with friends and church activities, a man she loved, and her children.

Maybe Raziq was right and this wish was more like a curse. Everything she wanted most was still out of reach.

She pulled the bottle stopper and the next moment, Raziq lay next to her, his legs crossed, eating a sandwich.

"Is that peanut butter and jelly?" she asked.

"Uh-huh."

"Pretty prosaic food for a magical being."

"Peanut butter and jelly, prosaic? Never. It's food for the gods."

Jasmine grinned at him. "I bet a lot of seven-year-olds will agree with you. Do you like Mc-Donald's, too?"

"Fast food is the pits. Swine eat better."

"Raziq, I need to tell you something," Jasmine said, her voice grave.

His eyes widened. "Gods, you're not going to tell me that Mickey D's is your favorite restaurant."

"No. It's not about food. I want to tell you that . . . I'm scared." Her eyes widened at the enormity of her confession. She'd never admitted fear before to anyone, not even her best friend Carmel, who was like family. Jasmine was always the tough one, the one who sucked it up, who never cried or showed anyone how much it hurt.

Raziq swallowed the last bit of his sandwich. "I'll always protect you," he said.

She cocked her head. "Always?"

"I apologize. I should have said that I'll protect you for as long as I can."

She nodded. Right now, being close to him was good enough.

The doorbell rang. She peered at her watch: 12:30 P.M. It must be the delivery man. Her friend in Atlanta, Carmel, often sent her little gifts.

"Should I go?" Raziq asked.

"No, it's probably just the UPS guy." She got up and pressed the button on her intercom. "Who is it?"

"Sharon, from the office."

Astonished, she wondered if the job had sent Sharon to check up on her. If they were ridiculous enough to go that far on a first call in . . . ? "Are you going to let me in?"

"Uh, okay. C'mon up." Jasmine buzzed her in and

pulled open the door a moment later. She blinked in astonishment when she saw Sharon already standing there with a bouquet of dark red roses. How had she gotten up here from the ground floor so quickly?

Then Jasmine spied a glowing red globe hovering close to Sharon's left shoulder. It was small, only a few inches across, yet it pulsed with inner light and sent cold chills down Jasmine's spine.

"Hi!" Sharon said. "I heard you were sick, and since I was passing by on my lunch break, I thought I'd bring these by to cheer you up." She proffered the flowers.

"Uh, thanks," Jasmine said, edging away from the red thing at her door.

"May I come in?" Sharon stepped toward her and the globe moved with her, looking as if it pulsed with anticipation.

"No!"

Sharon frowned.

"Are you all right?" Raziq called from the bed, sounding concerned.

"I'm fine," Jasmine said. She reached and took the flowers from Sharon's hands. "Sharon, I don't want you to get sick." She coughed for effect. "It's an awful bug; you really don't want to get it. Thanks for the roses, though; they're beautiful. Tell Tom I might be out for a few days." With that rush of words, Jasmine closed the door in Sharon's face.

She leaned against the door and listened. There was a pause before Sharon walked away. Even her footsteps sounded angry.

"What was that all about?" Raziq asked.

Jasmine reached up into her cabinet for an old wine carafe she used as a vase. "That was Sharon.

It's strange that she would show up here; we barely speak at work. And Raziq, there was this weird pulsing ball of light with her."

A frown creased his brow.

"That's why I shut the door in her face. I remembered what you said about how nothing could enter unless invited. I didn't want to let that thing in."

"You made a good decision. What you described is sometimes how human spirits manifest."

"Are you telling me that was a ghost?"

"Probably."

"What was it doing with Sharon?"

"Perhaps someone close to her recently passed away, but more likely, if you were wary of it, it's a lost spirit she picked up. They're attracted to certain vibrations."

Jasmine stuck the roses into the makeshift vase, taking care because of the long, huge thorns. The roses had the biggest thorns she'd ever seen. "I can't deal with this," she muttered as she filled the vase with water.

"Those are some big thorns," Raziq observed.

"I wasn't talking about the thorns."

He hesitated. "Then make your wish," he finally said.

She cradled her head in her hands. "I dunno what to wish. Damn, damn, damn."

"You need to conquer your fear. Fear attracts negative entities," Raziq said.

"Oh, I'm not supposed to be afraid of monsters flying in the sky and demons walking around hiding in people and globs of ghosts floating around?" she asked, incredulous.

"They won't hurt you. How many years have you lived? They haven't hurt you yet. Why would they start now?"

"You said they know that I can see them now."

"But nothing else has changed except they are more eager to prey on your fear. Don't let them."

She bit her lip and moved the roses to the kitchenette table.

"Get up and dress. Let's go out and get something to eat," Raziq said.

"Why don't we order in instead?"

"Don't be a wuss," he said.

"You're calling me a wuss? I'm not a wuss!"

He grinned. "Wuss," he said again.

"Take it back," she demanded, only half joking.

"Nope. Prove to me you're not a wuss." He threw a pair of jeans at her. "You're shaking in your shoes at a few minor demons and a harmless ghost. Shame on you."

Jasmine laughed. "Okay, let's go get some food. We need to pick up some groceries too, 'cause you've eaten up what little I had in the house."

She went into the bathroom to pull on her jeans and sweater and put on some light makeup. She felt better. She didn't want to consider how much her good feelings depended on Raziq's being around.

"You look good enough to eat," Raziq said as she came from the bathroom, his eyes lit with inner fire.

She bit her lip. "Don't say things like that to me. It makes it worse," she said, her voice soft.

"I'm sorry. But there are things that even a djinni finds difficult to control."

Jasmine closed her eyes momentarily, confusion flooding her. Pain and passion weren't two things she normally associated with each other, but Raziq's kiss and touch were both. Ecstasy and fire.

"Here's your coat," Raziq said, his voice grim. He draped her jacket over her shoulders. "Let's go."

She nodded, feeling claustrophobic. They needed to get out of this small and enclosed space.

She pulled open the door. The glowing red globe was hovering right outside and streaked past her into the apartment.

6

Raziq grabbed the roses, thorns cutting into his flesh.

"Too late," Jasmine heard a strange woman's voice say.

She wheeled to see a woman with hair so blond that it looked white. Her eyes were light gray, the color of ice. Pale skin covered sharp and regular features. She was mature and beautiful, clad in a black business suit. She held a carved glass bottle.

"Come to me, djinni. Ready yourself to serve your new master." The woman opened the bottle and drew a stick from her sleeve.

A magic wand? She had to be kidding. "Get out of my apartment," Jasmine ordered.

The woman pointed the wand toward her. "Impudent fool," she said, her voice dripping with disdain. "Prepare to die."

"No," Raziq roared, and her apartment exploded in fire and lightning.

Jasmine screamed in horror, and fire rushed into her mouth.

The next thing she knew, she was waist deep in noxious, stinging brown liquid. Raziq was next to her.

"What the—?

"Where are we? What is this stuff? It's awful," Jasmine said, trying not to panic. Endless silver walls curved upward into darkness and felt as if they'd crumple and collapse upon her at any moment.

"Shush," he said.

She heard the woman's cultured voice cursing and things being thrown around. "She's looking for us," Raziq whispered in her ear.

Finally, the apartment door shut and footsteps receded.

Raziq waved his hand and the liquid was gone. "I dared not use more magic while she was so close," he said.

Suddenly, Jasmine was dry and sitting on a white fur rug in front of a blazing fire.

"What is going on, Raziq?" she asked, her voice as calm as she could manage.

"We're in a can of diet cola, located deep in your kitchen trash can."

Okaaaay. "Your answer isn't helping me," she said.

"At the time, I thought hiding was the best way to elude the sorceress."

"Sorceress, huh? And you're telling me that brown stinky stuff was diet cola?"

"That's right."

She'd never drink diet cola again. "She's gone. Let me out."

"I will eventually. I hope," he added.

"You hope? Honey, you'd best *know* because I am not, *am not,*" she repeated, "spending the rest of my life in a diet Coke can!"

"You didn't tell me the globe was red—only that it was glowing. I assumed it was white," he said, his voice strained.

"What does the color have to do—?"

"If it were white, it would just be a harmless ghost. But red indicates demonic influence. And it, along with the red roses, was the gate for its master. The roses must have held an amulet that allowed evil inside."

"How would Sharon know that you were here?"

"You said that you didn't know her well. She might be an acolyte."

"An acolyte?"

"A practitioner of magic."

"You're telling me that Sharon is a witch?"

"Wicca is pretty specific and rarely evil. I only said she probably was a practitioner of magic. Considering her company, likely, sorcery."

Jasmine digested this. "Why did that woman attack you?"

"She wanted to capture me and harness my power for herself. If I'd left you, she would have used you as bait to get me and then would certainly kill you."

"Why does she want djinni power?"

Raziq rubbed his temple. "I sensed a nexus of dark magic rising in the world. But I never thought that so soon . . . This is bad, very bad."

A pack of Newports appeared in his hand and he pulled out a cigarette. "Do you mind?" he asked.

Jasmine shrugged. She had kicked the habit years ago, and smoke no longer smelled good to her, but she remembered well how it felt to crave a cigarette and not be able to smoke one.

"I really need to get out of here," she said, her

words echoing weirdly against the curved silver walls.

"We can't. The messenger demon is surely out there. The sorceress knows we could not have left the apartment. As soon as we materialize, she will be upon us."

"What's to keep her from simply taking the can of Coke?"

"She can't sense my presence once I'm enclosed. She must wait until we djinn are free of our bottles to gather us. She knows we'll emerge eventually. Those ones are patient."

"There's more than one?"

"There are many people who practice the dark arts. But it's rare that one gains such power. The last was called Hitler."

"Hitler!"

Raziq nodded, looking worried, and his cigarette ignited spontaneously. He pulled in a deep drag and exhaled. "Even that one never collected magical beings to increase his power. But he ushered in a darkness that lingers to this day. Only his hubris and poor decisions saved the world in the end. This one is worse."

Girly pseudo-Hitler was more than she could absorb. She was more concerned with getting out of a diet Coke can. That was more than enough.

"Are you telling me we can't leave here?" she asked.

"Time runs faster here. I'm hoping that someone will come to gather your things, and they'll take out your trash. I can mentally suggest to them that they retrieve the can. We can escape then."

"Everybody will believe I'm dead. Oh, Lordy, why?"

"You say that a lot. Clearly no lord is going to answer you directly."

"It's just an expression, Raziq."

"Yes, everybody will believe you're missing."

"But my job!"

"You don't like it anyway."

"I like paying my rent."

"Well, after you're missing for so long, I doubt that—"

She held up her hand. "Don't say it. Do you realize how hard it was to find a halfway decent apartment that I could afford in New York?"

"I'm sorry," Raziq said, exhaling smoke. "I can make you more comfortable." He waved his hand.

Jasmine blinked as it suddenly seemed as if she were sitting on the carpet in her own apartment.

"I took the liberty of adding some square footage," he said.

She looked at the drab beige carpeting, her dingy kitchenette, and used bed with the saggy mattress. "You didn't have to make it look like my apartment," she said. "I don't mind if you spiff it up."

"I thought the familiar surroundings would comfort you, but I can furnish it the way I usually do my own home."

"You mean the perfume bottle?" Jasmine asked, curious.

"That's right."

Suddenly, they were sitting on silky grass; flowers bloomed everywhere with small trees both budding and heavy with fruit at the same time. She looked up into sunny blue skies that curved down into walls.

"This is my garden. It doubles as a living room. Everything is artificial, of course, but it helps me feel freer."

"It's beautiful." She heard the babbling of a brook and walked behind a bank of blooming bushes to a creek that emptied into a deep blue pool.

"It's heated," Raziq said.

"Wonderful," Jasmine said, thoroughly bemused.

"Follow me." He walked to a portion of blue sky that opened like a door. Through it was a gym crammed with state-of-the-art exercise equipment. "The sauna is over there," Raziq said with pride.

An ordinary white door led from the gym. "That's the den," he said. "Follow me."

Jasmine peeked through the door and saw a wall with the largest plasma television she'd ever seen and banks of electronic equipment. There was a desk with an open laptop on it. Her eyebrows shot up as she saw that it had a wireless Internet access. Genies e-mailed? "What's your e-mail address?" she asked.

"RaziqDjinn@gmail.com. You're going to keep in touch?"

"Count on it," she said.

The area also featured a full wet bar and a cushy worn leather recliner that was positioned in front of the television. An exquisite Persian carpet covered the floor. Stars twinkled from faraway walls, and a low-hanging silver moon lit the room.

Raziq waved his hand and a dimmer switch appeared close to her. "You can control the moon's illumination from here," he said.

Jasmine squinted into the distance. Were those clouds suspended in the air?

"That's my bed," he said.

Her heart rate immediately increased. She realized that this seemingly huge space was going to seem small indeed. Black magicians, demons, and

mansion-sized diet Coke cans faded into insignifi-
cance compared with her need for Raziq. They
both stared at his bed of clouds. Jasmine shook her
head. At this rate they both were going to end up
cinders.

7

Raziq wished he could comfort Jasmine. He wanted to wrap his arms around her and bring her close . . . But close, he'd smell the traces of her namesake flower, which bloomed in the night and infected the air with its fragrance, as she infected him with this wild, sweet desire.

He'd not desired a human this way for millennia. When he first sensed her, he thought he was waking from a bad dream, that he was back in time and his Hyeth had come back to life and was calling him.

He could no longer remember Hyeth's face or her fragrance. His beloved wife was lost to the clouds of time, but Jasmine was here and now. Jasmine's features were as delicate and chiseled as fine lace, her eyes huge night pools. Her hair flowed over her shoulders like a fluffy ebony cloud, woolen and silk, and her lips, ah, her lips. God, she shone like the sun to him. She was unaware of her grace, her astonishing beauty, her winsome personality, and most of all, her effect on him.

No, he couldn't comfort her, he dare not touch her. She stirred up dormant and forgotten desires, futile desires. One wish from now he'd have to leave her forever.

"Raziq?"

He looked up and shook out another cigarette. He never smoked around a human—too hard on their delicate mortal lung tissue. But inside here with him, in non-corporeal form, the smoke couldn't harm her and the harsh menthol taste calmed his nerves.

"What are we going to do?" she asked.

What indeed. "The eleven P.M. news will be on in a few minutes. Wanna watch?" he said.

"Eleven? It was barely one a few minutes ago, when . . . it happened." She bit her lip, an endearing nervous mannerism. He admired her all the more for how well she was taking the fact her world had turned on end.

"Like I said, time is faster here," he said. "We're outside the boundaries of time and space. The longer you're in this dimension, the faster time goes inside here."

She swallowed. Then she said in a small voice, "I don't want to watch television. I think I'd like to go swimming in that pool."

He thought of her nude body slicing through the blue water. "Um, I'll stay here."

"Please come with me. It's irrational, but . . . I don't want to be alone."

She held out her hand and he was helpless in the face of her desire. He stood and waved his hand. They were at the pool. He couldn't help putting Jasmine in a two-piece thong made of glittering golden fabric. As his body reacted to her nearly nude form, he realized he'd made a mistake.

She looked down at her body. "What the f—"

"You look lovely," he said.

"I look like my ass is hanging out." With those words she dove into the water and hid the delicious view from his eyes.

She cut through the water like a mermaid. "Join me!" she called, treading water.

He dare not. The way he was feeling, they'd set the water to boiling. Literally.

He waved his hand, sat in his recliner facing away from the pool, and picked up his remote. "I'm going to catch the news." He conjured an extra large pizza with the works, a perpetually icy mug of beer and two frosty glasses. "There's food here when you want it," he called.

She swam to the edge and put her elbows on the soft grass growing there. "Why do we need to eat, sleep, etcetera, when we've shrunk enough to fit into a soda can?"

"We haven't shrunk, exactly, we've shifted. We are in a place, but we created a bubble, and within it is another dimension, another world, where we are essentially unchanged."

She looked confused and shook her head. She opened her mouth as if to question him further, then shook her head. "Okaaaaay," she said, and twisted to float on her back.

He averted his eyes from her stiffened nipples and pulled his mind away from his stiffening member. This was going to be tough. He piled up three slices of pizza on top of each other and took a bite.

He was halfway through the pitcher of beer when she approached him. "Uh, where's the bathroom?"

He waved his hand and a square white cubicle with an ajar door appeared. "The bathroom's right in front of you."

"Thanks, and could you give me my clothes back?"

With some regret, he nodded toward the bathroom. Her clothes were on a stool, laundered and neatly folded.

She'd shut the bathroom door behind her when he cocked his head and listened. There were presences in her apartment—some were men, but two women held his attention. One was older and one younger, their auras were dimmed with grief—mother and daughter. The younger one's grief lay heavy and black within, filling her. He reached out and touched her.

Not many humans knew that the djinn chose the humans they wished to grant wishes to, rather than the other way around. It had been many years since a human had stirred him enough for him to call them to release him from the comforts of his bottle. But when Jasmine walked into the shop that day, there had been something about her . . . He couldn't resist drawing her to his bottle.

When the woman returned to Jasmine's apartment, it would be time for them to go.

He was tired. He moved everything to his den, including Jasmine and the bathroom.

He conjured a salad for Jasmine, remembering how much she'd enjoyed the one at the restaurant. Personally, he thought raw greens a delicacy best left to livestock. He couldn't remember the type of salad dressing she'd ordered, so he provided an assortment.

She emerged from the bathroom, unfortunately

fully dressed, and blinked. "I hate it when you do that," she said.

"When I do what, move you or provide you with a meal and a comfy recliner to eat it in?"

"Moving me and disappearing my clothes. Both are disconcerting." She eyed the food. "The food part is great. I bet you live on pizza and PB&J sandwiches."

"Sometimes I have a steak," he said.

"Any vegetables, ever?"

"I have French fries and the occasional baked potato with my steak. Apple pie, too."

She laughed. Her voice sounded like bells ringing. She'd braided her thick, wild hair into a restrained single plait that hung down her back. He wanted to take it down and rub his face into its softness before he . . . Ahhh, he was going off the deep end over this woman. Drowning.

She served a big bowl of salad with blue cheese dressing. She looked around for a plate and he obliged. She stuck a slice of pizza on the plate, nestled to her salad bowl. He had to wrest his attention from her lips as she ate. God, he was watching her like a dog begging for meat.

Problem was that's pretty much what it felt like.

He pretended to watch television while he spent all his energy trying not to pay attention to the woman sitting next to him.

"I'm ready to go to bed."

Raziq flinched as if she'd slapped him. But he nodded, determined not to take his eyes off the television.

"Uh, could you join me?"

He gave her an incredulous look. Ye gods, the woman was mad.

"Not the same bed," she said hastily.

He was powerless in the face of her every desire. "All right," he said and turned off the television.

"Why do you do that?"

"What?"

"Use the remote control for the television when you can do anything with a wave of your hand. And why, why, why do you wear a Timex watch when you could have a Rolex or any other watch in the world?"

His lips twisted. "My Timex works."

He raised his hands and both were in their beds, a respectable ten feet from each other.

"Damn, I'm naked as a jaybird!"

She sounded upset. But he'd thoughtfully provided her with silk sheets. "You're covered," he said.

"Give me my pajamas. I hate that clothes-disappearing thing you do."

Ah, if she only knew all he wanted to do to her.

"That's better," she said. He'd clad her in a long yellow flannel nightgown. "What was that sound?" She sounded alarmed.

He listened and heard men's heavy bodies moving Jasmine's belongings, their deep voices rumbling. "Someone is in your apartment. Men are searching it. I presume to find clues to your disappearance."

"Already?"

"You've been gone for almost two weeks."

She frowned, discomfited.

He wanted to reach out and comfort her, but he was too close as it was. In all the centuries of his life, he'd never felt an attraction so strong. An age ago, he would've thought she'd cast a spell over him. But in this age, no magic could capture a djinni's heart, only his power.

"I told you time is faster in here," he said. He turned to his side, back away from her, and prayed to the old gods for sleep.

"You've never told me about yourself." Her voice was soft.

He turned on his back and sighed. A pang struck him, of loneliness maybe. Companionship and passion were things long denied him—and still were. He was one of a dying race. His age was over; his civilization had been destroyed by water and earth, retribution for their sin of almost destroying the home they'd be given, Gaia, the world.

He drew in a breath. Maybe passion could be only a memory, but for this moment, he had a companion. Why not talk?

"I have been in captivity for millennia. All the remnants of my people are enclosed in bottles or other containees, except for a few half-breeds who escaped, their blood now much diluted by the race of man."

He made the mistake of looking at her. Her lips were parted, the deep pools of her eyes fixed on him.

He moved his gaze back toward the cold, glittering simulations of stars above.

"War after war decimated our race and made a ruin of the earth. Men, humans rose from the ashes and the remaining djinn mated with them."

He heard her sharp intake of breath. "Their children, the half-djinn, reigned with fear and terror. They enslaved the people of earth and demanded their worship. Wars began anew, now between half-djinn and man. Man was on the verge of extinction."

He took a deep shuddering breath. "Then the earth heaved and cracked open. Waters flowed from the deep and poured from the heavens."

"Like Noah's flood," she said. He nodded and closed his eyes with the pain of memory.

All he'd known was swept from the world in what seemed like an instant. His wife and young children were swept away by the crushing wall of water before he could snatch them. His human wife and half-djinn children were lost, unable to save themselves. Ahhh, even now he could hardly bear his grief. He no longer remembered his Hyeth's features, or the smiles of his children. Even their names had fled into the mists of millennia. But he couldn't forget his love for them. The gods didn't grant so much mercy.

"My wife was human," he said. He shouldn't have told her that, but it slipped out unbidden. Something about Jasmine reminded him of Hyeth.

"What happened after the flood?" Jasmine asked softly.

He'd been silent, lost in his memories and grief, too long. "After the waters receded, everything changed. We became slaves of men, and mating with humans burned both djinn and human. We became bound to our containers, never able to leave and walk the world free as we once had."

He felt the bed of clouds shift. She'd moved closer to him and dispensed with the safety between them in an instant. She pulled the cover over herself and he felt her warmth. His body responded.

He lifted a knee and put his hands behind his head, effectively trapping them so he wouldn't reach for her. Staring upward, he kept talking. "A few half-djinn survived, snatched to safety by their parents. Half-djinn could leave their bottles if released by their djinn parents. Some djinn tried to keep their offspring captive because of loneliness and grief. If they did so, the half-djinn eventually died. So most of the few half-djinn who were rescued joined the humans. The last of fiery djinn blood walking free has been diluted by generations of mixing with the blood of humans. There were other races of fire and air, such as fairies and trolls. These races were also lost or only remnants remain."

"That's a sad story," she said.

"You need to get back into your own bed. The danger is real and there is only so much I can take."

"Sorry. I wasn't thinking."

Humans didn't think nearly enough. "The age of fire and air was long and prosperous. For the most part, the world thrived. It's only just past the dawn of the age of man and already your race is in peril."

Raziq watched the age of man playing out with weary eyes. Their wars were increasing in ferocity and breadth. They were ruining the world and poisoning their brethren, the other peoples of water and earth, before they even realized their existence. Rapacious and dangerous men rose to power, heeding only their greed and paying lip service to a form of godly devotion, unmindful of its power.

Another race was emerging, more malevolent than any he'd known before. Demons roamed the earth, their objective—the destruction of man. Human magicians joined with the demonic and in their rush toward glory and power, unknowingly hastened the progress of their civilization's demise. Legend said that war between demon and man would rend the world at the end of the age, and the defeat of man would mean their annihilation by fire. When the demonic finally overran the earth, the balance of the universe would be tipped irrevocably toward evil.

"You look upset," Jasmine said.

He glanced over at her. "Go to sleep. We have a full day tomorrow."

He had to figure out how to defeat the sorceress and the demons that controlled her. If the wars came before the appointed times, humankind was doomed.

He looked at Jasmine's small figure huddled under the covers. For her sake and the memory of his wife and children—his fate was set, his kind doomed, but humanity was just out of its infancy, and it deserved the opportunity to grow up.

8

Carmel Matthews walked with the detective away from her best friend's apartment. Jasmine had been missing a month. Her mind had gone over every scenario but always ended up at the same one and skittered away. Why would her responsible friend disappear with no belongings, no purse, no cash, not even her apartment keys for weeks and not contact her job and the people whom she considered her family?

"I hate to go back. Are you sure it won't make any difference if I stay? What if she comes back home?" Carmel asked the tall, austere-looking man next to her.

"She expects you to be home in Atlanta. We'll call you the moment we find anything new."

Her eyes filled. These past few days she'd been surprised by tears wetting her cheeks and stinging her eyes. Her grief was constantly leaking out.

"Thank you. Call me anytime, day or night."

Carmel clutched Jasmine's childhood photo album to her chest with one hand, and her purse held a beautiful antique perfume bottle, two things the detective kindly had allowed her to take from the apartment after the police had examined them. She knew that particular photo album was Jasmine's most precious possession. The beautiful perfume bottle would be a remembrance of her best friend. Her tears threatened to spill over.

The detective held the apartment building door open for her. She walked down the steps, feeling lost. How could she go back to her life with Jasmine out in this big city somewhere?

"Do you want me to hail a taxi for you?" the man asked.

"Thank you," she said. She had never gotten the hang of that particular New York thing. He raised his hand and soon a taxi moved to the curb. "Thank you for all your trouble," she said again.

He nodded at her. "Take care. And make sure you get home safely."

She settled back and only then noticed the diet Coke can in her hand. She must have carried it from Jasmine's apartment. Why would she do such a thing? She stuck it into her purse.

"Where to, lady?"

She didn't want to go back to her hotel, to enclosed walls and her lonely grief.

"Could you take me to Central Park?" She needed trees and grass. Fresh cold air. She'd take a walk. That would help make her feel better.

He dropped her off where there were plenty of people moving in the chill gray winter sun, walking their dogs and jogging.

She tipped him generously, then walked a little way, still cradling Jasmine's photos. She sank down on a park bench, the book on her lap. She drew the diet Coke can out of her purse and threw it into the trash can beside her, then opened the photo album. She smiled at the opening pictures of Jasmine and her family, a photo taken on a cruise they'd all taken together a couple of years ago.

A familiar voice cried, "Carmel!"

Carmel jumped to her feet, the photo album tumbling to the dirt.

Jasmine Flynn threw her arms around her and hugged her tight. "It's great to see you."

Carmel pulled away and stared at her. Jasmine was here, real and in the flesh. She wasn't dreaming or hallucinating. To her chagrin, she started to cry. "You're not dead," she said, digging in her purse for tissues, her voice choked with sobs.

Jasmine took the tissues from her and wiped Carmel's cheeks. "No, I'm not dead."

"You disappeared for a *month* without a word, and didn't take a damn thing. What are we supposed to think?"

Jasmine looked up in confusion at a handsome man standing close to her, brown skinned, with tight curls but indeterminate race and nationality. "I was gone a month?" she asked him.

"I swear I'd slap you silly if I weren't so glad to see you," Carmel growled. Jasmine had allowed everybody to think she was dead because of some man! She needed her ass kicked all over New York City.

All of a sudden, Jasmine's complexion turned ashen. "Oh no, God, no," she said, genuine terror on her voice. Carmel swung around and whipped out her cell phone, ready to punch in 911. "What's wrong? Who's after you? Is it him?" Carmel pointed to the man.

"I wish Raziq were human, I wish Raziq were human, I wish Raziq were human," Jasmine yelled, making the man flinch and Carmel drop her cell phone in surprise.

There was some sort of flash; it seemed like fire ignited out of the air for an instant along with the sharp smell of ozone.

"What the hell was that? What's wrong, Jasmine? I don't see anything!" Carmel was whirling in circles, adopting a fighting stance.

Jasmine drew in a trembling breath. "It's gone, thank you, Lord, it's gone."

The man looked aghast. "What have you done?" The man's voice was wild and he ran his hands through his hair in agitation. "What in the names of the gods have you done?"

Carmel picked up the photo album out of the dirt and stared at the two of them. Had she entered the twilight zone? She needed some Excedrin or a stiff drink. Maybe both.

9

Blood pounded through Raziq's veins, deafening him. An ocean of air pressed down, crushing him, while a fearsome silence rang in his ears. He rubbed his eyes, blind, unable to see anything but the earth, blue skies, humans, and their creations. He gasped, icy air filling his lungs. Ye gods, it was cold.

"Raziq, are you all right?" Jasmine asked him, her hand on his back.

He realized that he was crouched over. He straightened. "No, I'm not all right." He focused on her face. "Woman, what have you done to me?"

"The question is what have you done to her?" the woman interrupted, her voice loud and angry. "We all think she's dead and it turns out that she's off gallivanting with you."

Jasmine opened her mouth and Carmel raised her hand. "That is not like you, girl. What has this man done to you? You don't call us, you kiss off your job and disappear? What?"

The woman glared at Jasmine and she only shook her head.

"The hell with this," the woman said. "I'm calling the police."

"Don't," both Jasmine and Raziq said together. Raziq raised his hand to disable the woman's phone temporarily and then stared at his hand in consternation. He felt no power, no nothing. He was no longer able to manipulate the energies, waves, and particles of the world with his will.

Nausea rushed through him. "I think I'm going to puke," he said.

"Is he on drugs, Jasmine?" the woman asked.

"Are you sick?" she asked, staring at him with worry.

He nodded, rubbing his eyes with his hand, trying not to bend over and heave the contents of his stomach on the ground.

"We'll all go back to my place," Jasmine said. "Then I can explain, Carmel . . . or try to."

"It's not safe," Raziq managed to get out.

"Where are we supposed to go?" Jasmine asked.

"Everybody thinks you're dead!" the woman yelled, causing Raziq to squeeze his eyes shut. Gods, she sounded like a banshee on the loose.

"And you're standing out here carrying on as if, as if . . ." Her voice trailed away. "Shit, I need a drink," she muttered.

"Me too," Jasmine said.

"I'm going to die," Raziq said, feeling that he indeed might keel over at any moment. Gods, *gods,* the woman had wished him human.

"Who the hell is he?" Carmel demanded.

"He's Raziq," Jasmine answered.

"You're in trouble, aren't you?" Carmel asked. "Is he really going to die?"

"I think he's just fluish. I guess I am in trouble," Jasmine said. "But it's not what you think. I've done nothing wrong and neither has Raziq."

"We have to go," Raziq said to Jasmine. He focused on Carmel. "For your own safety and that of your family, I advise you to keep silent about seeing us."

"What is going on, Jasmine?" Carmel demanded.

"Would they hurt her?" Jasmine asked, fear edging her voice.

Raziq nodded. "They would hurt anybody."

"Would who hurt me? Jasmine, what is he talking about?" The woman started to cry again.

A feeling of helplessness swept through Raziq. Gods, he was human and he was going to die in a few short years. That is if he were lucky. He could die today or maybe tomorrow. He peered around and felt a shiver go through him at being unable to see the entities that shared the world. He needed to get inside. He felt too vulnerable out here. "We need to go," he said.

The woman stuck her chin out. "She's not going anywhere with you," she said.

"I have to go with him, Carmel," Jasmine said. "I couldn't live with myself if anything happened to you or your family."

"Is he the reason that you disappeared for almost a month? Without a call, without a call, Jasmine! How could you do this to us? To me?" Tears continued to roll down Carmel's cheek, and Raziq saw Jasmine tremble.

"I'm sorry. I'm sorry. Please understand that I'd never want to hurt you. That's why I have to go now. And that's why you have to be silent."

Carmel wiped her cheeks with the back of her hand and sniffed. She lowered her head, then nodded. "Okay. We've been girls for a long time. I will trust you know your business and I'll mind mine. But if you need money, anything . . ."

Jasmine was embracing her, also crying.

It was touching, but Raziq felt an intense need to get out of the open. He moved toward the street and raised his hand to hail a taxi.

A taxi zoomed past him and Raziq put a cigarette in his mouth, then remembered that he couldn't light cigarettes any more with a flick of his will.

He pulled the cigarette out of his mouth, stared at it, grimaced, and threw it the trash can. What about those dreadful diseases humans got? Gods, he was going to have to stop smoking.

A taxi finally pulled over. "Jasmine," he called.

She pulled away from her friend and ran to him, her face wet with tears. He stood aside and let her in first.

"Where to?" the driver asked.

"The Ritz-Carlton, please," he said to the driver, naming the only hotel he'd ever stayed in, oh, seven or so decades ago.

Jasmine wiped her face. "You got Ritz Carlton money? That's no small dime," she said.

He pulled out his wallet. He was fairly sure that his brethren hadn't left him broke and homeless in the human world. He flipped open the wallet and found credit cards, a birth certificate, and driver's license with the name RAZIQ DJINN on it. Not very creative. A bank account. They'd given him an identity and money, so that for the short time until he died, he'd survive as a human. Kind of them.

"I can take care of it." He stared out of the window at the utter blue emptiness of the sky. He was scared; he felt like crying; the urge to kill Jasmine for her crazy wish crossed his mind; and most of all, he was dying for a cigarette.

As soon as their taxi pulled up to the hotel, Raziq tipped the doorman a hundred dollars, and slapped down his credit card on the front desk. "I'd like the best suite available and please establish an account."

He waited while they checked his card and credentials. Then, as he expected, once they gauged his wealth, the tenor of their service changed.

"Of course, Mr. Djinn. May we take your bags up to the room? The maid will unpack for you."

"No bags," he said. "We'd like to get to our suite as quickly as possible."

A few minutes later Raziq threw himself across the bed of their palatial suite.

"Are you still not feeling well?" Jasmine asked. "Can I get you anything, call room service?"

"Not right now. I need some rest. Why don't you go downstairs and get what you need. Have them bill it to our hotel account." He closed his eyes and exhaled in relief as he heard the door close after her.

Jasmine seemed pleased about his transformation. She'd whispered in his ear in the taxi that the demons were gone.

He knew that they weren't gone. He hadn't told her how he personally preferred seeing what was out there. He'd never mentioned how he liked having the power to use the energies around him to transform molecular and atomic structure with his will. He'd kept silent about how the idea of living for millennia agreed with him, and how being able to smoke a cigarette would make him a happy man. He hadn't said a damn word.

Jasmine had snatched his life away with three
sentences and thought she'd done him a favor. He
closed his eyes to the beginnings of an aching
throbbing at the back of his head and temples. So,
that was what a headache felt like.

He rolled to the side of the bed, picked up the
phone, and punched the button labeled ROOM SER-
VICE. "Aspirin or whatever you people are taking
for pain nowadays."

He considered ordering a fifth of Jack to wash it
down. He had a fondness for human whiskey, but
now the stuff would tear his liver to shreds. The
human rules seemed to be to take however good
something was and multiply it by desire and that
equaled the harm it caused the human body.

So far, it sucked to be human. He was dying
every moment, but he was determined that he
wasn't going to help the process along.

Even though he was human, he did have some
control over his fate. Raziq closed his eyes and
concentrated on his breath, floating his consciousness on the movement of it, in and out, in and out.
Eventually he reached that in-between place where
even a human could go. There were no thought,
no worries, no fear . . . nothing between him and
the infinite oneness but peace.

A knock at the door jarred Raziq back to his
present. His headache was gone, along with his
feeling of panic.

He took the small bottle of white pills and Perrier
and tipped generously without allowing the man
into the room. He could not discern the true na-
ture of other humans yet, but he soon would.

Lying back on the bed, he closed his eyes again and slipped more easily into the place of eternal consciousness and waited for what he might soon know.

Raziq opened his eyes. The scent of night blooming jasmine teased him. She was close. "I thought you'd never wake up," she said, her voice throaty.

"I wasn't sleeping," he said.

She tumbled on the bed next to him and snuggled against his body like a warm kitten.

Ahhh, Jasmine. His arms tightened around her and drew her close. He inhaled the sweet scent of her hair. What was it about this woman in particular that moved him so? Her body type wasn't his preference; she was far too skinny. But somehow it didn't matter. Her beauty shook him to the core. She could be abrasive and she was guarded, nontrusting. But all he wanted to do was protect her and be with her and no other.

This was the woman for him. There was something about her. Almost as if he knew her from long ago. It made no sense but it was as if she were Hyeth. But Jasmine was herself and no other. It disturbed him profoundly that she carried what he remembered as Hyeth's aura as if it were her skin scent.

He couldn't resent her for the wish that had profoundly changed his world. She wanted him to be safe, to be happy. She wanted to make love to him.

He watched her lips, full and delicious, like crimson fruit. Desire filled him, like slow honey dripping from a comb. Delicious. He moved and claimed her lips. They were perfect, juicy pomegranates, ripe to bursting. Her mouth was soft, her passion blazing.

The fires between them no longer literally burned, but they were no less hot.

He rolled her over, learning her honeyed mouth, his tongue exploring its sweetness, and pinned her to the bed with his body. She melted, her legs opening, her soft center grinding against his hardness.

He said a word in an ancient language, long dead, and thrust against her, gently rocking against her most sensitive part. She hissed through her teeth.

He undid the button at her collar, rotating his thumb through the fabric on her hard nipple with his other hand, not stopping the roll of his hips against her.

He couldn't wait. He pushed up her shirt and bra and gazed at her high round breasts, small and perfect. "Beautiful," he murmured. "You're so damn beautiful."

She smiled up at him. "So are you."

He grinned and kissed her lower lip, giving it a little nip. "Men aren't beautiful," he said.

"Some women might disagree," she said.

He circled his tongue around one erect nipple, then the other. She sucked air through her teeth.

"I want to give you what you desire most," he whispered, his hand unbuttoning her jeans.

She stiffened at his words, her temperature plunged. "What did you say?" she asked, frost in her voice.

He raised a quizzical brow. "I said I want to give you what you desire most." He thrust at her for emphasis with a grin, trying to regain the mood. "This."

"Get off me."

He drew back and stared at her, incredulous. "What?"

"Get. Off. Me."

He moved off her. "Did I hurt you?"

"It felt like you did," she said, her voice choked.

He was aghast, and visually checked her body for bruises. Was it possible that he didn't know his own strength? "Where are you injured?"

"I'm not injured." She got up and sat on the side of the bed, facing away from him. "You don't have to make love to me because I wished you were human. Accepting a mercy screw isn't my style."

Raziq drew in a sharp breath. "Are you blind and deaf, woman? Have you not seen and heard how much I want you?"

"That was before. Now, you're out of danger. You said it yourself; you want to give me what I desire most—you. You think I wished you human because I wanted to . . . you know."

She moved from the bed and stood, crossing her arms, still not meeting his eyes. "I don't deny that's what I wanted, but I also wanted you to be safe from that awful sorceress person, and I wanted those damn demons out of my sight. There was something that looked like a giant flying snake headed for us in Central Park. It was the most awful thing I've seen in my life—and recently I've seen more than a few awful things."

"Jasmine," he said, moving toward her. She backed away. He bit back a curse of frustration.

"Don't get me wrong," she continued. "I'm happy you're human and everything and I'm willing to help you get established in your new life. But I don't want you doing anything for me because you're grateful or feel beholden to me—"

"Shut up," Raziq said. Jasmine's mouth snapped closed and she stared at him with narrowed eyes.

"You have no idea what you've done to me," he said, starting to pace. "I was virtually immortal compared to fragile humans. I had power over the things of the world, and I could smoke a goddamn cigarette!" He paused and closed his eyes. *Breathe,* he reminded himself.

"You made me human," he continued in a calm, low-pitched voice. "I understand your reasoning behind your wish. But you truly have no idea what you've done. I am staring Death in the face—" He bit off his words. He didn't want to rage at this woman and most of all, he didn't want to show his fear.

"I need to get out of here." Raziq put his hand on the doorknob and hesitated, remembering all that was out there that he could no longer perceive. "Shit," he said, backing away from the door, his hands falling to his sides in defeat. "I'm afraid to go outside." He rubbed his eyes. "Fear is not an emotion with which I'd ever been so intimately acquainted."

He glanced toward Jasmine. She stood like a statue, a stricken look on her face. Regret replaced some of his fear. He wanted to banish her sorrow and ease her mind, not make things worse for her.

She didn't resist when he drew her into his arms. "I shouldn't have lashed out at you," he said. "You were only doing what you thought would help."

Her fingers curled into his T-shirt, and she buried her face into his chest. "No, I'm sorry. I didn't think. I should have asked you, discussed it . . ."

"What's done is done," he said. "Hey, there is an upside."

She pulled out of his arms and he felt bereft.

"Don't joke," she said. "You have no identity, no job. How are you going to live? I didn't think. Please forgive me." She dropped her head.

He dared move a step closer. "Remember when I told you that our powers are pooled to grant a wish?"

She nodded.

He pulled out his wallet and handed it to her. "How do you think I got this room? I have money, a driver's license, and a birth certificate in there." He drew out a key to a safe-deposit box. "I'd bet anything my diploma, transcript, and passport are in that safe-deposit box also. My brethren wouldn't abandon me."

Her face brightened. "You have money?" She sank back down on the bed and examined the contents of his wallet. A glint of a smile played across her face. "Raziq Djinn, huh? You'd think they'd go with Smith or Jones, something inconspicuous like that."

"They didn't have a lot of time."

"No, they didn't." She handed back his wallet. "I feel better now. At least you don't have to worry about that sorceress or those demons capturing you."

Raziq sighed and ran his fingers through his hair. All he now had to worry about was being killed. But why add to her fears right now? She was sure to have fear enough in the coming days without his doing a thing.

10

Jasmine's eyes widened when she saw the balance at the end of Raziq's bank statement. One hundred million dollars! The man had a hundred mil—*poof!*—just like that. She mused on the amount as she followed Raziq and the banker to the safe-deposit box. He could do anything, go anywhere. Have anyone. She didn't miss the appreciative gazes that constantly followed him.

Yet, no matter how much he denied it, he would feel obligated to her. He knew that her wish couldn't be altruistic and he knew exactly why she wanted him to be human. *I want to give you what you desire most.*

Her eyes closed involuntarily at the memory. Words didn't encompass how much she desired the man. Lord, she hyperventilated and probably drooled every time she was in his presence. But a man that fine didn't live millennia without knowing his effect on women. Oh Lord, he wanted to give her what she desired. The very thought made her skin heat in the sterile atmosphere of the bank.

She bit her lip. On one level she wanted Raziq more than anything, no matter what, but on the other hand, she didn't want him on any other terms but love and commitment.

She knew that anything else would tear her up. Her heart bruised easily and it could take no more beatings. Raziq had the potential to land the mother of all technical knockouts.

No, she couldn't tolerate his touch out of pity or obligation, or even mere sexual desire. He needed to have a chance to make his own choices, like any man. A man such as he was, wealthy, so handsome he could be called beautiful, caring, and pleasant, once he saw what was available to him in the world . . . why would his choice be her?

She'd topped her hill and was edging down, defeated and torn down in the love department. She cared enough about Raziq to want better for him. Better than her.

He'd been trapped in a little bottle, no matter how luxuriously appointed, all alone for millennia, interrupted only by the occasional human eager for him to grant a wish. The thought of his being captive, a slave to wills other than his own, upset her.

Genie or not, there was a wildness to him, a confidence, self-possession and comfort—she couldn't imagine Raziq being a willing slave to anyone.

Then add in that crazy sorceress running around trying to enslave him every time he peeked his nose out of his bottle, and Raziq had to be better off. Granted, being changed to human had been unexpected. It would upset anyone, throw anyone off balance. She imagined that it had been a profound shock to Raziq's system.

The improvement of his state had to sink in eventually. He worried about dying, but she was certain humans had souls, an ever-after that genies possibly couldn't share.

She took a deep breath, resolved that she'd help him all she could, and then let him free and allow him to fly as a man, all on his own.

"I have a favor to ask you," Raziq said. He'd finished gathering documents out of the safe-deposit box.

He nodded toward the bank official. "He tells me that my old friend is available. I need to go and meet with him."

"You have an old friend here? I thought you said you hadn't been out of your bottle for decades."

"He's not human. He's half demon. I heard he recently married a human and settled down."

"Half demon? The demons I saw were awfully . . . ugly."

"Trent was born before the flood. He was one of the few demon-human hybrids who survived. He's a pretty nice guy, but the demons made it pretty rough for him until lately."

Her face heated as she realized Raziq was staring at her lips. He leaned in to whisper into her ear. "When you're deep in thought, you bite your lower lip. Very sexy. I can't wait to get you back to our hotel room." His voice was drenched with chocolate liqueur, and suddenly Jasmine wanted to drag him to the nearest ladies room, climb on up, and have her way with him.

Being with Raziq, human or not, was going to be hard on her, whatever way she looked at it. How was she supposed to turn down his advances when she had to frequently stifle the urge to tear off his clothes and jump his bones?

"The bank also helped me arrange a personal shopper to come here and assist in getting us the basics. The people here are extraordinarily helpful."

"Hundred-million-dollar depositors tend to bring out helpfulness in a banker," Jasmine said.

"You could tell them your size and preferences, go with her or him if you like or return to the hotel. I'll be a few hours."

"That's okay. What size are you?" she asked.

He shrugged. "Guess, all right? I need to get going. Have them get me some jeans and T-shirts, and a warm jacket. I'm freezing all the time now."

He dropped a light kiss on her lips as if he were a familiar lover and strode away. She watched him go, touching her lips, full of longing.

Damn that man.

The secretary ushered him into the huge corner office. "Raziq!" Trent said, getting out from behind his desk. "Good to see you out of that damn bottle." He reached out to slap him on the back and froze in the middle of the movement, astonishment crossing his patrician features. "You're human. How the hell did that happen?"

"The woman who opened my perfume bottle wished it."

"Really? Well, it's good to see you anyway. Please sit down." He motioned to the leather couch in the corner. "What can I do for you?" he asked.

Trent would have made a perfect James Bond.

He was dark and patrician, with swaggering good looks and the prerequisite British accent. He flipped open a box on the coffee table and drew out two fine cigars. He handed one to Raziq.

Raziq opened it, smelling the aroma of fine tobacco with pleasure. Trent ignited the ends of their cigars spontaneously. Raziq suppressed a touch of melancholy at the loss of his own powers.

"How about a drink?" Trent asked.

"Scotch and water will be fine."

Raziq decided to get right to the point. "A sorceress is capturing djinn to harness their power. A blonde. Heard anything about it?"

"I don't travel in the circles where I can receive the latest news anymore. But I've heard of someone, a new and powerful tool."

"A woman?"

"Yes. I wouldn't be surprised if she is doing as you say. She has the attention of the highest princes, and her will and power are beyond the ken of the average human."

"If she's in the service of the princes, you know what I fear?" Raziq asked.

"I fear the same." Trent handed him his drink, then sat adjacent to him and pulled out his wallet and showed Raziq a photograph of a beautiful woman with raven hair and sky blue eyes holding a baby. "My son," Trent said.

"Congratulations."

"Thanks. I have to protect him from his own these days. My demon kin seek to kill him."

Raziq frowned. 'Why? Are the demons so jealous that they begrudge your happiness?"

"I'm of no importance to them, my wife less so—it's my son they are after."

He took the photo from Raziq and studied his child. "Our son is Chosen, one of those who will stand with men at the final battles."

"But if the war is started too soon by this sorceress's will . . ."

"Humanity will die unfinished, doomed and without rebirth . . . along with my wife and child."

Trent handed him a drink and they sat in silence for a beat.

"Is she very beautiful?" Trent asked.

"She is to me."

"I have not seen that look in your eye since Hyeth. Once a human becomes that precious to you, it changes everything," Trent said.

"Your memory is keen. My memory of Hyeth's eyes has faded into the mists of time."

"Forgetfulness is often a blessing, and memories are sometimes a curse," Trent said.

Raziq gazed into the golden fluid in his glass. Over the millennia, he had discovered the wisdom of living in the moment. Now his moment was Jasmine. Why was she precious to him? There was no rational reason because he'd only known her for what he considered an instant of time. She simply was.

Raziq took a puff of his cigar. "I have to stop the tool."

Trent nodded. "They won't be able to raise another to such power for decades, and by then the appointed times will have come and gone. But how can you stop her?"

Raziq stubbed out the cigar in the ashtray. It had been good, but now he had to put the enjoyment of such things aside. "I don't know. There has to be a way and I'll find it."

"My wife's guides tell her that my destiny is to protect my family, my child. I can't leave. But I'll assist you all I can."

"The woman I'm with saw her face."

Trent studied his drink, as if searching for answers within. "The tool thinks you're a djinni cowering in your bottle. She believes you're not a threat and hers for the taking as soon as you emerge. But she'll certainly want to destroy the human who witnessed the truth of what she is."

"I know. And I can see nothing, nor protect her from nothing."

"The demons will be eager to find and expose her to curry the favor of the princes. You must ward your woman carefully."

"I'm weak and helpless, human." Raziq studied his hands, human, but once capable of shaking this skyscraper to its foundations by a mere movement.

"Don't underestimate humans. That is where other races made their mistake. That's the reason why they are no more or dying—including the djinn. And that's the mistake demons are going to make. You're human, but you can do more than you think. You can protect her. She can protect herself. Humans can fight demons. My wife saw the truth of it. It's what the demons fear most and why they are trying so desperately to kill the Chosen while they are vulnerable. Humans have the power to kill them."

"But how?"

"I'm not sure. But the spirits may know."

Raziq stood and walked to the window, gazing out at the tall man-made buildings. "I want to meet with your wife. She can consult with her spirits and show me the way."

"It's not possible. It would endanger our son on several levels. The exposure is simply too great a risk."

Raziq nodded. "I understand."

Trent took something out of his desk drawer and handed Raziq a leather necklace that held a small bag of probably unidentifiable substances. "A charm," he said. "It will keep her safe until you discover your path."

11

Raziq hesitated, then knocked on the door of Jasmine's hotel room. He hated that Jasmine had insisted on separate rooms, but chose not to make it an issue.

The television was on, but she looked sleepy-eyed, as if she'd woken from a nap.

"I got some good news and some bad news," he said. "Which do you want first?"

"The bad news." She preferred to get the worst over.

"We need to keep moving. The sorceress thinks I'm inside the bottle, so she's not looking for me. She's looking for you."

"Why is she bothering with me? I can't do anything to the woman!"

"You know what she is."

Jasmine swallowed. "We can't keep running and hiding indefinitely."

"No, but here's the good news. We're going to take her out."

"What do you mean 'take her out'? Kill her? Do

you recall that lightning stuff she threw? How she appeared out of nowhere? You don't have your fire to throw anymore. You're human."

"And that's exactly why I can defeat her now. Trent says that there's a way. Now all I have to do is discover it."

"It's a little much for me to absorb, Raziq."

"I understand. Here, take this." He handed her the charm.

She wrinkled her nose without touching it. "What is it?"

"It's something that will protect you from demons and magical attacks until we figure out how to defeat the sorceress."

"It looks and smells like a little bag of rat poop."

"You need to put it on."

"You're joking."

He shook his head. "You've seen what's out there, and in what numbers. This is not the time to joke."

She grimaced, but put on the necklace charm without another word.

"Did you get what you need?" he asked.

"Yes! I almost forgot." She rummaged though some packages and held up a lambswool-lined suede jacket.

"Nice." He reached for her, to give her a friendly hug, but she eluded him. Just as well; there was no time for dallying.

"We need to leave this city."

Jasmine nodded. "I don't want to tangle with that crazy woman—especially now that you can't get me back into a diet Coke can."

He stifled a sigh. Helpless definitely wasn't his preferred style. "Do you mind buying two tickets, first class. We need to leave within a couple of hours max. Do you have your passport with you?"

She shook her head.

"Too bad." He handed her a charge card. "I'm going to return to my room and order in a meal. Are you hungry?"

"A little."

"I'll order something for us and have some luggage delivered. You'll be over in say, a half an hour?"

Jasmine nodded and sucked her teeth. Her life had turned topsy-turvy and she didn't see it getting straight anywhere soon.

Exactly two hours later, Jasmine sat in first class looking over an inflight magazine on the way to Atlanta. She'd decided if she could go anywhere she wanted, that would be to see her peeps. Raziq wasn't too happy about it, but said it would probably be okay as long as they didn't stay long.

The plane taxied to the runway and paused, waiting for clearance to take off. Jasmine noticed tenseness radiating from Raziq. The plane accelerated, pushing them slightly back into their seats. His cheeks were pinched and ashen while his hands gripped the armrests as if holding on to the plane for dear life.

Dang, her ex-genie was afraid of flying. "Don't fly much, huh?" she asked.

"Nope."

She covered his hand and he intertwined his fingers with hers. His hand tightened as they became airborne and earth fell away.

Jasmine stared out the window until she saw the gorgeous view of New York as they curved around the Statue of Liberty. "Look, this is my favorite part," she said.

Raziq snorted.

"It'll be all right," she said, giving his hand a squeeze.

"Are you sure? I mean, trusting in the inch or so of metal between my ass and fifty thousand feet of empty oblivion below, seems to take more faith than I can presently muster."

"A funny genie."

"I'm no longer a genie and nothing about this is remotely funny."

"It's safer than driving in a car. Honestly," Jasmine said.

He cocked his head and looked at her. "At the brisk rate that you humans transform yourselves to the semblance of hamburger within your cars, somehow your assurance fails to make me feel better." He caught the eye of the flight attendant. "Scotch and soda; make it a double."

"What would you like to drink, ma'am?"

"Some white wine would be fine."

The stewardess soon returned with their drinks in real glasses. First class had its perks, Jasmine thought as she twirled the stem of her wine glass and luxuriated in the wide, comfy leather seats.

"Do you realize how many of my liver cells I'm getting ready to destroy, some irreplaceably?" Raziq said as he tipped his glass.

Jasmine shook her head.

"Too damn many. A human liver is a wondrous thing. So are the lungs. But gods, what I'd do for a cigarette."

"Oh, I forgot." Jasmine rummaged in her purse and pulled out a box. She tore off a small square of gum and handed it to him.

"What's this?" he asked.

"Nicotine gum. It'll really help your cigarette cravings."

He squinted at it. "Do you know what this substance does to the cardiovascular system—"

"No. And I don't want to. Put it in your mouth and chew it."

He sighed and obeyed. He drained his glass and settled back in the chair.

"What's happening to me is beyond my experience," he said. "And, to be frank, I'm not caring for it much."

"You'll get used to it. I guess genies don't turn human every day."

"Lucky buggers."

"Buggers?"

"It's an expression," he said.

"Isn't being human better?" Jasmine asked. "We have freedom."

"You've been listening to too much American propaganda. Your concept of freedom is pretty much a myth and thus highly overrated."

Jasmine couldn't understand him. He had free will now. He could go where he felt like, do what he wanted. "Don't humans have perks, too, that make us better than other sorts? We have souls."

"Better? A touch ethnocentric, aren't you? Everything has a soul. I had a soul as a djinni. Nothing really ever ends or dies; it's simply transformed."

"So why did you say you were afraid of dying then?"

"Like most humans—djinn, fairies, demons, elementals, and the like don't particularly look forward to dying, either."

"I can relate," Jasmine said. "Generally we humans try not to think about it."

He shifted in his chair and motioned to the stewardess for another drink. "I can't figure out how you manage it. Death is hanging over you continually, ready to strike you down at any moment. You're defenseless from it."

Jasmine sipped her wine. "Now you're the one not being very reassuring."

"Sorry. The perk that humans have is their fecundity. Many die and many are born at any one time. You've spread to almost every corner of the earth. You're constantly rebirthing yourselves, recycling your souls." He cleared his throat. "Many liken your race to cockroaches and say humans will be the ones to inherit the world forever because it's too difficult to completely eradicate them."

Jasmine frowned at him, offended. "Cockroaches! Thanks a lot."

"Cockroaches are cunning creatures, fecund, and they live everywhere and anywhere, with amazing endurance and adaptability. They're the ultimate survivors. I consider the comparison a compliment."

"I don't. They are filthy creatures, leaving droppings of their wastes everywhere. I hate cockroaches. I want to hunt them down and kill them whenever I see one."

"Some races feel exactly that way about humans . . . most notably demons."

Jasmine shuddered. "They're still all around us, aren't they?" she asked, her voice lowering to a whisper.

"They've grown amazingly numerous on earth recently. Prophecy says their objective is to wrest the earth from human domination."

"What prophecy?"

"You're not familiar with prophecy? The threads of truth that run through every canon of the world, within every nation, ethnicity, and every religion? The stage is being set for the final war between demon and man, and the fate of the world will lie in the balance. My world was destroyed by water. Prophecy states that yours may well be destroyed by fire."

Jasmine stared out the window, thoroughly freaked out and not really wanting to hear more.

"Therein is the danger of the sorceresses," Raziq continued. "They believe they're duping and controlling the demons to obtain power. Those humans don't realize that they're merely pawns of what they fail to fully understand and the instruments of the downfall of their own race. The demons call them *tools*."

Jasmine cleared her throat. "How can you stop them? What hope do we have?"

Raziq touched her hand. "There's always hope; there's always a way out. That's how the universe works."

"Do you know what you're going to do next?" Jasmine repeated, not bothering to hide her fear.

"No, I don't know. I have to remain open to guidance and trust in the wisdom of the universe," he said.

Jasmine rolled her eyes. "Yeah, right. I have a hell of an easier time trusting that this plane is going to stay up in the air until it gets ready to land."

Raziq was silent.

Demons, monsters, and ghosts, oh my, Jasmine thought. This wasn't her style at all.

Raziq closed his eyes and retreated into himself for the rest of the flight, unmoving even when the plane landed, bumped along the ground, and taxied to a stop.

"We're here," she said.

His eyes opened immediately, his gaze clear and alert.

She stifled a yawn. It'd been a long day. She stood to retrieve their carry-on luggage. "As soon as we get off this plane, we can rent a car and head out to Carmel's."

"You know we can't stay," he said, as they moved with the crowd of people off the plane.

"I know. I just need to touch base, that's all."

When they entered the crowded airport, Raziq stopped and scanned the airport crowd with narrowed eyes. "What's wrong?" she asked.

"Auras. I'm seeing some auras around a few people again. It's as though I am completely blind, and tiny flashes of light are flickering through the darkness."

"I don't know what auras are. Are they scary?"

He glanced down at her. "Not at all. They are the energy matrix around everything that holds it together and defines it. A human aura is like a fluctuating halo of light in various colors surrounding the body. I can try to train you to discern them if you like."

"Uh, no, thanks." The last thing she wanted to be trying to do is see more freaky stuff.

He grinned. "C'mon, loosen up. Hurry up and call Carmel so we can go and pick out our car."

A few minutes later, Raziq told the car rental rep who'd reeled off the makes, models, and colors of the cars on hand, "I'd like to see what you have on the lot."

The young man was short and had what looked to be prematurely balding patchy brown hair and ruddy skin. "That's not really necessary, sir."

"I think it is," Raziq replied with a smile. The man grumbled under his breath, irritated, and picked up the phone to get somebody to take over the front desk.

"I wonder if he has gnome blood," Raziq whispered in Jasmine's ear.

Raziq bounded out of the car as soon as they arrived at the rental car lot. He pointed at a gleaming silver BMW Z4. "That's the one I want."

The car rep blinked. "Are you sure?"

Raziq nodded. "Yep."

"It's quite expensive."

Raziq raised a brow at the man. "So?"

After what seemed like a mountain of paperwork, the car rental rep handed them the key to the chosen car, and Raziq slid behind the wheel with a grunt of satisfaction.

He put the key into the ignition and expectantly grasped the steering wheel.

"Aren't you going to start the car?" Jasmine asked after a few moments.

"Is there a special word to say or a button to push besides putting the key in the hole?"

Oh, Lawd. She unhooked her seat belt. "Trade seats. Looks like I'm doing the driving."

"It's all right. Just show me how to do it."

"I can't just show you. It takes time."

"We have time."

"Raziq! Remember what you said about hamburger, humans, and cars?"

"There is that." He got out of the car, holding the driver's side door open for her. "It's all yours."

The car handled like a dream as she whipped down the highway. She wished it were warm enough to put the convertible top down. Expensive car, fly man at her side with virtually unlimited funds. She was getting way too used to this.

"It doesn't look that hard," he said.

"One wrong move and we're fodder for Mickey D's."

His eyebrows shot up. "Uh, drive carefully."

"Always." It was great to be back in Atlanta. At the moment, she had no idea why it had taken her so long to come back home.

12

Jasmine pulled into the circular drive of Steve and Carmel's large brick suburban home.

"Nice house," Raziq said.

All of a sudden, she had a vision of a house just as large, but with a Victorian look surrounded by land, rolling hills, and trees. *Their house?*

Lawdy, she was losing it. Jasmine wrenched her mind to the matter at hand, took a deep breath, and rang the doorbell.

"Aunt Jasmine!" A pretty young woman pulled open the door and fell into her arms.

Jasmine embraced her, then stepped away, surveying her at arm's length with a grin. "Melanie, I can't believe how big you've gotten the past year. You're a full-grown woman."

"Yep, a college woman. Hey, I pledged."

Jasmine whooped and made the shake. "How's your first year at Spelman treating you?"

"It's sweet. Steve and Mom relented and let me move on campus after winter break. C'mon in!"

Melanie drew her inside and Raziq followed.

"Who's he?" Melanie asked, giving him a look a hair short of a glare. "So it was true? You let us all believe you were dead while you ran off with some man?"

Jasmine shifted. "No, it wasn't like that."

Melanie relaxed. "See, I told Mom it was crazy. I knew you had a perfectly logical explanation."

"Jasmine!" Carmel's son, Trey, came barreling down the stairs. "I'm real glad you're not dead," he said as he bent over to hug her shoulders. She'd never get used to the six-foot-four version of Trey.

"I'm glad I'm not dead, too. How're you doing, baby?"

"I'm doing fine. Who's he?"

"Trey and Melanie, meet Raziq Djinn."

Trey and Melanie eyed Raziq.

"So you brought him anyway," Carmel said, before either of her children responded.

"Carmel," Jasmine said, "be polite," she warned. "It's good to see you, girl." She looked around. "Where're little Stevie and Blossom?"

"They're asleep. It's almost ten, way past their bedtime. Steve's on call and in surgery. He won't be back until later. Y'all hungry?"

The food smelled like home. Carmel could throw down in the kitchen.

"Very," Raziq said.

"I'll just have some coffee." The stresses of the day had totaled up and Jasmine needed the caffeine.

A few minutes later they were all seated around the kitchen table: Trey, Melanie, Jasmine, and Carmel, with Raziq focused on his plate heaped with tender brisket, new potatoes, greens, and macaroni and cheese.

A bittersweet feeling of déjà vu struck Jasmine.

If only she could wind time back six or seven years and undo her mistakes.

"Steve and I ran into Keith at a party last weekend," Carmel said, stirring her coffee slowly. "He said he was here in Atlanta to stay."

Jasmine's lips thinned. "We both figured that."

"There's more. He's married again, Jasmine."

She studied the black coffee in her cup, afraid to speak, afraid that her voice would betray the sudden fury that burned within. "Good for him," she finally said.

"Since you're back to stay in Atlanta, I thought you should know. I wanted you to hear it from me," Carmel said.

"It's okay. It's a closed chapter of my life." As she uttered the words, she realized that they were true. Keith had been nothing but a waste of her time. What she had left was fury, disgust, and disappointment in herself. How could she have been such a fool? He had made her wait six years fueled with nothing but promises and lies, then as soon as he was free, married someone else.

Tears stung her eyes at the enormity of the waste.

"Baby, he isn't worth two thoughts from you," Carmel said.

Raziq lifted his head. "She's right, you know."

"I'm not worried about him. Lately, I've had far more pressing stuff on my mind." Jasmine gave Raziq a troubled look.

Melanie and Trey looked at each other, uncomfortable with the turn in the conversation.

"I have class tomorrow; I'd better get to my bedroom," Melanie said. She gave Jasmine a quick and fierce hug. "You take care of yourself. We love you."

"I love you too, baby."

" 'Night, Aunt Jasmine," Trey said, dropping a kiss on her cheek.

" 'Night. Be good boy."

"Always."

"The kids look as if they're doing well," Jasmine said after Carmel's children had left.

"They are. Melanie is doing well at Spelman, and Trey got accepted to several Ivy League universities, but he's decided to stay here and attend Morehouse. I'm proud of them both."

"You should be."

"This food is great," Raziq said, looking up from his plate.

"Carmel can throw down in the kitchen. She's one of those belt-loosening cooks."

"There's plenty of food. Are you sure I can't get you something, Jasmine?"

She couldn't imagine eating. "No, I'm fine."

Carmel cleared her throat. "I think it's time that you two let me in on what's going on," Carmel said. "What sort of trouble are you in?"

"It's nothing like you think," Jasmine said.

"Why didn't you want to return to your apartment? Why didn't you report whatever happened there to the authorities?"

She darted a glance at Raziq. "And who the hell is he, really? Do you realize how much trust I've laid on our long friendship to allow him into my house with my children?"

What was she supposed to tell her friend? Jasmine wondered. Demons, monsters, and ghosts wouldn't wash at all with Carmel.

She cast a pleading glance at Raziq, but his gaze was fixed on the small kitchen television.

She looked to see what he was watching and

gasped. A blonde woman was having what appeared to be a press conference. "Oh my Lord, that's the woman who attacked us!"

Carmel turned around and looked at the television. "You gotta be joking."

Jasmine shook her head.

"That's Adrianne Dimontas, the woman the Senate just approved for Secretary of State."

Raziq's brow creased and he pushed his plate away.

Carmel's eyes narrowed. "Y'all must be in bigger trouble than I thought."

"We all are," Raziq said.

Carmel looked troubled. "I don't know if I want to hear any more. Nothing's more important to me than my family, my children."

Jasmine moved over to her and put her arms around her friend's shoulders. "I understand. We aren't asking you to involve yourself in anything."

"If you need any money . . ."

"No, we don't need anything. Raziq has resources."

"Are you a spy or something?" she asked Raziq. "What mess have you involved Jasmine in?"

Raziq's fingers tapped the table. "I'm no spy, and neither is Jasmine. We aren't enemies of the state or wanted by the law. But you were right when you said you don't want to know. Believe me, you don't."

Jasmine nodded. She knew for a fact that if they started talking about demons, Carmel would have a fit.

"Thank you for the meal; it was lovely. Jasmine, I had no idea she had so many in this house, young children, too. It would be better if we left."

"I know you wouldn't bring any danger or threat into my house—to my family," Carmel said to Jasmine.

"No," Jasmine said. "No, I wouldn't." She stood. "Goodbye, Carmel. Give Steve my regards and the kids my love again. Kiss the little ones for me, all right?"

Carmel also stood and pushed her chair carefully back to the table, not meeting her friend's eyes. "I'll see y'all to the door."

They followed her out of the kitchen, silent, nothing else left to say. Jasmine opened the door and raised her foot to step through when Carmel called, "Jasmine!"

Jasmine turned to face her friend. "If you need anything. A place to hide, any amount of money. Let us know. We're your family and we always got your back, no matter what."

Jasmine nodded, her eyes glistening with unshed tears. Then she stepped through the door. When it closed behind her and Raziq, it felt as if a part of her past had closed and fallen away.

She squared her shoulders and walked out to the car by Raziq's side, prepared to face her new life. "Where are we going?" she asked.

"A hotel. We're beat. Let's get a good night's sleep, and we can catch a plane in the morning."

"Catch a plane where?"

"Somewhere away from here. You're too easily traced back to your hometown. I should never have allowed you to come in the first place, but I saw your desire—"

"And as always, you wanted to give me whatever the hell I want."

"That makes you angry? What more do you want from me?"

Jasmine wiped at the corner of her eye brusquely, before the tear could fall. She wanted fairy tales, everlasting love and happily-ever-after endings. She wanted something that couldn't possibly exist. *Especially for her.*

"You've done more than enough for me."

"I haven't done nearly enough. I never meant this to happen to you. I only wanted to give you your desire, not rip the trappings of your life away."

There was nothing she could say. Her prior life was gone. But this one . . . despite all the craziness, the danger, the fear, something sparkled about the moments in her present. She was more alive than she'd been for years, perhaps had ever been.

She spied a Holiday Inn and turned in. It would do for the night. She turned off the ignition and they sat unmoving, unfinished business lying heavily between them. The silence was tense and boded a future so sinister and uncertain that Jasmine hesitated to break it.

"I'm sensing truths about what the future may hold. It started on the plane," Raziq finally said.

Jasmine remained silent, waiting. "Maybe it's this thing called intuition. All I know is that some things seem very right as some others seem very wrong." He turned toward her. "Being with you always seems right. It's the way it's supposed to be."

She didn't resist as he drew her into his arms. Heat simmered within Jasmine's veins running like hot melted chocolate to her inner regions. His arms tightened around her and her breath quickened. She ached to lift her head and feel his kiss branding his essence into every cell of her body. She wanted him so much.

And he wanted her. With one move, he could be hers. How was she supposed to resist this man?

Maybe you aren't, a treacherous voice whispered. She surrendered and tipped her head back, gazing into his handsome face.

His gaze smoldered and firm, mobile masculine lips lowered to meet hers.

A horn blasted behind them. Jasmine looked out the window at a car driving past them; they heard screeching tires and saw the driver's middle finger defiantly raised in her direction.

"He must have been waiting for our parking space," Raziq said.

"I'll go and get a room."

"Please get two rooms," she asked. He looked at her, a question in his eyes. "Please," she repeated softly.

He hesitated, nodded, and closed the car door behind him.

Jasmine lay her hot forehead against the cool steering wheel. She was falling in love with the man and there wasn't a damn way she could stop herself.

13

A soft tap at the motel door woke Jasmine. She knew it was Raziq. Her stomach tightened and her face heated and awareness tingled through her body at the thought that he was so close to her, mere feet away. All she had to do was open the door and lead him to her bed. Oh God, he wanted to please her and she needed it as much as she needed—Jasmine cut the thought short and threw back the covers. "Yes?"

"Jasmine, I've got tickets. We need to leave within the hour. I have breakfast. Open up."

She stiffened. His voice splashed her as if it were a cool water. "Uh, I need to shower and dress first." She leaned against the door.

"I'll wait. Let me in."

"No! Just give me fifteen minutes." Grabbing her robe, she scurried to the bathroom. She turned on the shower right to the edge of cold and dropped her nightclothes to the floor and climbed in. She flinched against the cold burn of the water. She

wanted Raziq so much, she felt as if she were
stretched as tight as a strumming wire or a tight-
rope . . . if she moved, if she reached out, if . . . oh
Lord, if she took what she wanted, she could fall.
She would fall and then she would crash against
the ground and break—again. How could she expect that any man would hold her tight and firm?
She'd lived almost half her life and no man had
ever come close.

Jasmine took a deep shuddering breath and
picked up the soap and washcloth. She'd do what
she had to do to get through, to survive. The memory of her mother's voice rose in her mind. *Take
every moment as it comes, do what you need to protect yourself and your heart, and girl, you'll make it on through.*

"Salt Lake City? You bought tickets to Salt Lake
City?" Jasmine said to Raziq after she handed the
keys to the rental agent and they walked to the
tram back to the airport.

"Why not?"

"I thought you wanted us to lie low, not stand
out. Do you know how many black folks are on the
street in Salt Lake City at any given time? I don't
think more than two are allowed."

"I'm not black."

Jasmine gave him an exasperated glance. "In
the U. S. of A., you're black, believe me."

"Give Salt Lake City a chance. I have a good feeling about the place. We don't have to stay long if
you don't want."

Her feeling of unreality increased. She was flee-
ing from demons with an ex-genie who'd been
human only a couple of days. Alrighty then. Their

destination did recede in the scheme of things once she pondered the entire picture.

Later, seated in first class, Jasmine opened a paperback novel she'd picked up in the airport, looking forward to digging into the book. The other passengers still filed by her seat.

Raziq stared out the window, still tense about the idea of flying through the ocean of air in a monstrous man-made contraption. Humans couldn't even make an automobile drive without any special training to operate the damn thing, and their cars still crashed into each other like bumper cars at a carnival.

A slim young woman with brown hair stopped beside Jasmine's seat, holding up passengers behind her to irritated murmurs. The woman stooped down over Jasmine, getting into her face. The seconds extended into moments, yet the woman stared, unmoving. Jasmine looked into the woman's face, irritated, and saw that the pupils of the woman's eyes were dead white, as if something were crawling behind them. Jasmine froze in terror.

Raziq looked toward Jasmine. An icy trickle of fear made its way down his back. Alarms sounded in his body and sirens rang in his ears. The woman housed a demon; he was sure of it. He had to do something *now*. But how could his frail, puny human self battle this creature? His mind clicked through the possibilities as rapidly as a calculator and Raziq realized his only course of action. He closed his eyes and instantly fell into meditation, then deeper into a trance.

Raziq knew that humans could separate their bodies from their spirits at will. Few could do it in practice, but the capacity was there. He was once a djinni, practiced in the mysteries. He had to do it to save Jasmine from the demon. Once his spirit was free from the flesh, he could confront the demon.

Then as he envisioned it happening, it did. His spirit moved out of his body, and the spirit turned to face the demon.

The demon, a bloated white thing, dug its tendrils into Jasmine's body, its evil intent evident. It was going to kill her.

He became aware of a familiar feeling. Power moved all around him, winding through the ethers, power that, as a djinni, he could collect and use.

He drew the power into himself. It worked! He felt the buzz of energies igniting his spirit chakras, flaming within him. He directed it toward the demon with a flick of his mind.

Fire slammed into the creature, burning it. It screamed a hideous howl, detached from Jasmine, and turned to face this new threat.

It whipped a tentacle toward him, streaming whitish gray flares of energy. Raziq felt the icy sear of it touch his astral body and jumped through the thin skin of the airplane still sitting on the ground onto its silver wing. The creature followed, snapping its whiplike tentacles.

Raziq circled the creature in the air, exhilarated to be free of his heavy human flesh, and to be able to grasp ethereal energies again. He raised his hands and the inrushing energies shook him, flooding him with power. He grinned, and raised his hands, shooting lethal streams of astral flame. The creature howled in agony as it burned.

* * *

The passengers screamed as the woman next to Jasmine crumpled to the floor. Jasmine was slammed to her seat, while something that felt like icy tentacles painfully dug through her ribs.

She couldn't scream and could barely breathe, much less move. She managed to direct her eyes toward Raziq, but it appeared as if he were unconscious. Coldness worked its way into her veins and she felt it wriggling wormlike through her brain. *Raziq*, she shrieked in her mind.

White mist moved in front of her eyes, shapeless and barely there. "Die, human animal," hissed a voice reverberating through her mind.

That was when she started to pray. Tears wound down her face, leaving trails of ice on her cheeks. She felt her heart flutter and beat erratically. Finally, her heart wrenched with an agonized twist and vibrated, no longer beating. Her body felt like so much meat, the pain receding. The light started to fade to black.

She had no preception of time. After what was either an eternity or a few seconds, she saw a flame in the darkness, illuminating a long tunnel. She started to walk, then run, scared, but excited. Somehow Jasmine knew that her family was waiting for her at the tunnel's end.

Then fire slammed through her and she heard a horrible voice screaming in agony.

Her eyes opened. She was in her first class plane seat, her novel discarded in her lap. Her heartbeat was regular, her body warm. She was alive. She touched her chest to check for puncture wounds. That was the worst nightmare she'd ever experienced.

The woman who had collapsed in the aisle next

to her was being picked up and carried out by paramedics.

Jasmine reached out with a shaky hand to Raziq. But his eyes were closed and he slumped forward in his seat, unconscious.

Raziq circled the plane, feeling free, his vision cleared, his power restored. He ignored the pull of the silver cord that attached him to his body. Then he felt Jasmine's panic as if she'd called him. He reentered his body.

She was shaking him, tears streaming down her cheeks. "Raziq, wake up, oh God, please. Raziq."

He opened his eyes and his gaze met her tearful one. "It's over, baby," he said. "I killed it."

"What happened? What just happened here? Are you telling me that was no nightmare? It was real wasn't it?" she asked, her voice high pitched and tremulous, telling him she was on the edge of hysteria.

"We need to go." Raziq stood and grabbed her hand. She needed no urging, but hurried to the front of the plane and out of the gate, past the passengers who were still waiting to reboard. The woman was on a stretcher, a look of confusion on her face.

"She'll be all right now," Raziq said. "The demon is dead. I killed it."

Jasmine half ran beside him in an effort to keep up with his long stride. He wanted to slow down for her, but some intuition spurred him to hurry. They needed to get out of this place.

"You were unconscious," she said, breathing hard. "I thought it got you, too, and you were dead. How can you say you killed it?"

"I left my body and crossed into the astral, the realm where the demons dwell in the flesh."

"What?"

"I'll explain later. But it's what Trent said I needed to find out, the way humans can destroy demons. Jasmine, I did it!"

They'd reached the airport exit. Jasmine's lips were pinched together, the expression on her face both exasperated and terrified.

"Don't you understand? If we cross over, we're more powerful than they are. It's what demons have feared all along—that numbers of humans realize demons exist along with their own capacity to destroy them."

"Raziq, all my life, you know, the life I had before I met you? I never gave demons a second thought. No, I take that back—I didn't give them a first thought, either," Jasmine said.

"That's how they like it." Raziq headed toward a taxi. "Let's go," he said, taking her hand.

Jasmine pulled her hand away. "Where are we going to go, Raziq? Where in this entire world are we going to be safe from creatures like . . ." She trembled and started to cry.

He raised her chin and wiped away a tear with a tender finger. "I will keep you safe, I promise you. Trust me."

She sniffed and wiped her eyes with her sleeve.

"Let's go," she said. "Almost getting killed by a demon can rattle a girl."

"No doubt," he said and took her hand again and led her to the closest taxi.

He stared out the window, deep in thought. A car dealership was coming up on the right. "Hey, pull in there, will you?" he asked the taxi driver. They needed to take the road. The airport being enclosed and crowded made them too vulnerable to detection and demon attack.

The car salesman irritated Raziq to no end, wanting to show him car after car. The man seemed eager to dicker about the price, the whole ordeal extending the process unnecessarily.

Impatiently, Raziq pointed to a silver Toyota 4Runner. "I will pay whatever is on the sticker for that car plus 10 percent added to your commission, if you can hand me the keys to that car within thirty minutes."

"But, but—"

Raziq looked at his watch. "Your time starts now."

The man literally ran back to the dealership.

"Think he'll have it ready in time?" Jasmine asked.

"The way he ran, I'm sure of it."

Thirty minutes later, Jasmine was turning onto the highway in the new car. "You have a thing for silver," she said.

"In cars, apparently."

"Where are we going, Raziq?"

He was silent for a moment, allowing his intuition to lead him. He'd discovered that human intuition was one of the most powerful weapons in his arsenal. It was as if the universe whispered through him, telling the right way to go, revealing all its secrets, if only one could become still enough to listen.

"Southwest, head southwest," he murmured.

Jasmine's lips tightened as she took the exit. "I need to turn around."

"Fine. And Jasmine—"

She glanced at him.

"Thanks for trusting me."

She sighed. "I don't see how I have much choice. Are you going to tell me what really happened in that plane?"

"You were attacked by a demon," he said.

She took a deep, shuddery breath. "It was the most terrifying thing that's ever happened to me."

"I doubt that anything more terrible has happened to many humans than a direct demon attack."

"I didn't say it was the most terrible; I said it was the most terrifying. Nothing that could happen to me would be more terrible than when my family died."

"I know the feeling," he said in a quiet tone, thinking of his family of so many millennia ago.

She was silent for a moment. "It was incredibly malevolent. It hated me and it wanted to kill me as painfully as possible. How was that woman a demon? She looked ordinary on the surface."

"No, she was possessed and controlled by a demon. When I killed the demon, I freed her. Demons are immaterial on this plane and can't directly affect matter. It had to invade your body to attack you and disrupt your energies."

"Are you telling me that it moved from her to possessing me? That quickly?"

"Yes, it did."

"So you're saying that any demon can just jump into me?"

"Not generally. There usually has to be an opening. It's like coming into your home—you have to invite it in. I don't know quite what happened in this case."

"How did you kill it?"

"I crossed over to the astral plane."

"What?"

Raziq grinned at her, "You say that a lot?"

"I don't think I say it enough, since I understand very little of what the hell is going on."

"Fair enough. The astral plane mirrors and overlies this one but on a different level of matter, a different dimension, you could say. Beings live there. Some exclusively, and some, like demons, live between both worlds, but in different forms. Humans sometimes get lost there immediately after death, or visit there in their dreams. Sorceresses often visit and draw power from that plane."

Jasmine blinked.

"You're dying to say 'What?' aren't you?" Raziq said with a chuckle.

"Nope, I'm dying to hit you," she muttered.

"Pay attention to the driving. We don't want to be hamburger. You can hit me later."

"Is that a promise?"

"I promise all sorts of hands-on sweaty action, although hitting is generally a little kinky for my tastes."

"Quit it," Jasmine said. "You were telling me how you fought and killed a demon while looking suspiciously as if you'd fainted."

"I concentrated the energies from the ethers—"

"You left your body behind and went to a different dimension, boom, like that?"

"I assumed you'd take good care of my body." He waggled his eyebrows. "Seeing how much you like it and all."

"Oooh, you really want to get hit. I should pull over and—"

He touched her face, her skin wondrously soft. "Yes, I really want it," he said, his voice husky.

Jasmine swallowed, not taking her eyes off the

road. "Quit it," she repeated, but her voice held no fervor.

"Never."

She stilled, unmoving. He wondered if she even breathed. He felt guilty. His sexual overtures were hardly fair considering all she'd been through. He'd been accustomed to demons for millennia. She was only now becoming acquainted with the creatures.

"Back to the demon fighting," he said. "Demons live on both planes. They are material, solid in the astral plane, while a human in the astral plane is constructed of the ethers you call spirit. Humans are more similar to demons than I knew. They do have the ability to cross planes consciously."

"So you are telling me I can leave my body and go to some other dimension where demons live in the flesh?"

"With training and practice, maybe. I believe I was able to do it because of my experiences and knowledge as a djinni combined with my terror for you."

A frown creased her brow. "But how did you kill it?"

"I blasted it with elemental energies. I have an affinity toward fire, so it's easy for me to absorb. Humans can also access the energies directly in astral form. They can concentrate them and use them to destroy the demons. I'm sure that's one reason that the demons endeavor to keep their reality secret."

"What's the other reason?"

"If the majority of humans believed in tangible evil, demons, conversely they would also believe in angels and possibly even the Most High."

"Most people do believe in God in some form."

"No, they don't. Not really. They believe with their lips, not their hearts. They have forms of godly devotion, but do not get the sense of it and remain unaffected by its power."

"I don't agree. My mother certainly believed. I believe."

"If humans saw the reality of the universe, it would likely mean the utter destruction of evil, since on the balance, most humans wouldn't choose evil willfully—although some would."

"So why don't angels show themselves? Why won't God?"

"The reasons are in your own holy books. There is an issue at stake for the souls of men, and has been since their dawn."

She swallowed. "You are saying that God cares more about an issue than us?"

Raziq shrugged. "I wouldn't presume to know."

Jasmine bit her lip.

"You will teach me to kill demons?" Jasmine asked.

Raziq heard the fear and uncertainty in her voice and wished he hadn't told her so much, so soon. But it was too late for regrets.

"Only if you teach me to drive," he answered.

"Deal."

14

If it were up to Jasmine, they wouldn't stop driving until nightfall and they were safe in a hotel room where demons couldn't invade past the doorway. Raziq kept reminding her that he needed to eat. She didn't want to go through the drive-through where demons lodged within the eyes of a human could jump out and attack. All she wanted was to burn rubber down the highway, maybe indefinitely.

"Jasmine, I'm starving. See that chicken place coming up? You have to stop." Raziq's tone of voice told her he wasn't playing about his food.

She sighed and turned off at the exit. She eased through the drive-through. "Do you think they would think I was crazy if I said I'd push the money under the door if they bring the chicken out, set the bucket on the ground, and back away?"

"Yes, they'd think you were bonkers for sure. They wouldn't do it, either."

"I think we should stock up on food now."

"I'm not trying to come down with food poisoning from spoiled food. I want three pieces white, fries, and a root beer."

"I know how you eat. I'm not stopping every couple of hours."

"Don't worry. I sense we're almost there."

"Almost where?"

"I don't know, baby. It is as it is."

Jasmine rolled her eyes. She ordered the food, and rolled up and proffered the money, thinking all the while, what a pain all this mystical crap was. And as for demons . . . she'd pay money to have them fade back into mythical creatures.

"Here, take the food." Jasmine thrust Raziq the sacks the boy at the window handed her. She pulled away from the drive-through window.

"Don't fret," he said. "We're almost where we need to be. Take the next exit off the highway, go right, and then make a right at the next road."

Jasmine drove over an unpaved road to a newly tarred driveway in the rural Georgia countryside. "Turn now," Raziq said, urgency in his voice.

She twisted the wheel and the 4Runner's tires threw gravel in the air as she made the sharp turn. "This is probably somebody's private drive."

"I know."

"Let me give you a news flash about Georgia. Folks driving up on people's private property are apt to get shot, particularly us brown-skinned variety."

"You worry too much."

"You gotta be kidding. A few hours ago I was attacked and almost killed by a demon. I'd say I don't worry enough."

"Baby, you have to admit that you are breathing now. Look, there it is!" Raziq pointed to a stately stone home in a grove of pine trees surrounded by what must have been an eight-foot-tall stone wall.

A youngish black man looking to be in his thirties with two dogs leaned against the wall and straightened as they approached.

He moved to their car and Raziq rolled down his window on the passenger side. "Can I help you folks?" the man asked.

"Is there a woman here?" Raziq asked. "I have the feeling I need to see her."

Jasmine closed her eyes, waiting for the man to tell them to get off his property before he got out his nine, or since this was the country, his rifle. To her astonishment, the man only nodded and said, "Bless said you'd be showing up. C'mon in."

They followed him through the intricately worked wrought iron gates. Jasmine noted that he shut the gate securely behind them and locked it. The house was built of solid gray stone with white trim, large but had the appearance of a welcoming and cozy cottage. Smoke curled to the sky from a fireplace, and two porch swings graced a wraparound porch.

A woman appeared on the porch, plump and dark-skinned, an infant in her arms and a toddler clinging to her dress. But as they drew closer, she smiled, and Jasmine was struck by her voluptuous beauty. The woman exuded peace and quiet confidence, a quintessential earth mother type.

"I've been waiting for you," she said, glancing at her watch. "You're right on time."

Jasmine's jaw dropped as she entered further into the twilight zone. Raziq only nodded.

"My name is Bless," she said. "And my husband Rick, my daughter Glory, and newborn Rick, Junior."

"Ricky," the man said. He reached out and shook Raziq's hand. "It's good to meet the parents of another Chosen One."

Deeper and deeper. "Neither of us has any children," she said.

Rick looked at Bless, surprised.

Bless shrugged. "Not yet."

"Follow me," Bless said. "I'll get y'all something cool to drink. Iced tea?" She turned to lead them into the house.

The woman had said she and Raziq were to have children. The words drove all thoughts of iced tea from Jasmine's mind.

"Are you coming?" Raziq asked. Jasmine realized that everybody was staring at her, including the baby.

Raziq held out his hand, a lopsided smile on his face. His face was so dear that her eyes filled. This was not the sexual urge that dried her mouth and made her ears pound with the beat of her heart so often. It didn't have a thing to do with how he looked, but how he was—caring, funny, tender, protective.

She put her small hand into his, her trust and faith freely given. Their fingers intertwined: a promise. He lifted her hands and kissed them. She knew as clear as a bell chime and without a doubt that what passed between them was far more precious than anything her body offered.

Bless beamed. "Fear is nothing but an illusion, see?"

They followed her inside to a large but homey room with exposed oak beams and a soaring ceiling and the biggest stone fireplace that Jasmine had ever seen. Big logs crackled with cheery firelight. Bless motioned them toward the sofa. "I'll get the iced tea and then we'll talk."

"I'm going to take the kids to the playroom," Rick said.

"Thanks, hon," Bless said as she left the room.

"How do you know her?" Jasmine asked Raziq as soon as Bless had left the room.

"I don't. I was drawn here and she was expecting me. Chill. Right now all is as it should be."

Jasmine leaned her head back on the couch, the feel of Raziq's hand in hers stabilizing her. She inhaled. Exhaled. "What drew you here?" she finally asked.

"The Universe, the greater Good, the Most High, I'm not sure what you would term it. The thing that permeates all things and holds the world together. That's the closest I can get to it, I think."

Jasmine closed her eyes. She wouldn't ask him what he was talking about again. Nope, she wouldn't. She would just sit back on this nice leather couch and breathe. In and out. Just think, mere years ago, she would have snorted her rum and Coke out her nostrils if anybody had told her that she'd choose to be with a New Age-type guy of her own free will.

"Here's your tea." Bless emerged with three tall, glasses of delicious-looking tea on a tray along with an icy pitcher. "I'm a Southern girl, so it's sweet tea. I hope that's all right with you."

Jasmine smiled. This she could understand. "I'm a Southern girl myself, from Atlanta."

"What're your names?" Bless asked, handing Raziq a glass of tea.

"My goodness, we didn't introduce ourselves. I'm Jasmine Flynn and this is Raziq Djinn." She stumbled over the words, realizing for the first time that their names rhymed.

"Nice to meet you Jasmine, Raziq." Bless handed Raziq his glass of tea. "The spirits say you have only just arrived from a faraway land?" she asked him.

He took a sip of his tea. "Further away than you

can imagine. Somehow I think you can help me solve the puzzle I'm working on."

She settled in a soft, buttery leather chair adjacent to them. "And what puzzle is that?"

"I need to destroy a powerful sorceress protected by legions of demons. She seeks to kill Jasmine. On the trip down, a demon attacked Jasmine but I managed to kill him."

"That's extraordinary. You crossed over while conscious with no training?"

He nodded. "Who trains the humans?"

Bless raised a brow. "You speak as if you're not human yourself. But I can see clearly by your aura that you're quite human, and a mage, too."

"I've only been human a few days. I was a djinn."

"That's a new one," Bless said, her eyebrows raised.

"I wished him human," Jasmine said. "What do you mean he's a mage?"

"He has much power within him," Bless said. She looked at Raziq. "You asked me how humans train to fight demons? I can tell you only how I trained— in one of the spirit realms, trained by spirit guides."

"How do I find my way to a human spirit guide?"

"You don't; they find you. But I don't think that's necessary. You were directed here for a reason and I was directed to watch for you. I think I'm to complete your training."

Raziq nodded. "I'm meant to defeat the sorceress."

"You're meant to protect the Chosen One. That's always the reason a parent is a demon slayer."

"A Chosen One? A parent?" Jasmine said, eyes wide.

"The Chosen are the ones of power who stand

against the demon hordes in last days, the battles of Armageddon."

That explanation deserved some more sugary tea and some aspirin, too, Jasmine decided. She had started with a genie, graduated to a sorceress, moved on to demons, and now they were working in Armageddon and the end of the world. Yep, Bless was way too deep for her.

"You need to prepare yourself. To be the mother of a Chosen One is a great honor but also a burden. The demons are desperate to kill them while they're vulnerable, while they are children."

"I'm thirty-six years old, and I can't have children."

"You may be thirty-six years old, but you're mistaken about the other."

Her pronouncement struck Jasmine speechless.

Bless stood. "We need to get started. Jasmine, I will work some with you later, but it will be quite boring to watch Raziq and me. It will seem as if we're simply unconscious. I'll show you to your room and you can relax."

Jasmine followed Bless. The room she ushered her into was pleasant with a queen-sized bed and a television. Bless's husband had already put their luggage by the bed.

Bless smiled at her. "Make yourself at home." She started to head out the door and turned. "It'll be all right. Don't worry."

"How did you know that we were coming?" Jasmine asked.

"I dreamed it and a little about you and your partner. Not much, enough to recognize you and let me know what I needed to do." She looked around the room. "Are you comfortable? Can I get you anything else?"

"Um, I'm okay."

"There's a bathroom through that door." She pointed. "Rick's probably in the playroom or the kitchen if you need something."

"Thanks a lot. I appreciate your hospitality."

She smiled at her again. Her smile was as pleasant and warm as the sunrise. "No trouble at all. In these critical times we will need to help each other more and more."

Jasmine nodded then looked away, her teeth catching her lower lip. "What you said about Raziq and me parenting a child disturbed me."

"I could tell."

"How can you tell that I'm the mother? He's a man who could have whomever he wants."

"Your aura is dimmed, gray with pain, regret, and most of all, fear. There's a cliff where you suspect your ultimate happiness is at the bottom, but you have to jump. You've taken the first step and now you're awaiting the painful, deadly plunge to the bottom."

Jasmine wondered how Bless understood exactly how she felt. There was something otherworldly about the woman. "A better word than suspect is hope. I'm hoping that my ultimate happiness is at the bottom, but too often my hopes have turned up empty and based on fantasy."

"Keeping trusting your heart and everything will be all right. Love is never wasted and if it goes out, it'll always come back to bless you." With those words, Bless left the room, shutting the door behind her.

Bless obviously had never met Keith. What a waste of love that man was. Jasmine put her iced tea on a coaster on the bedside table, kicked off her shoes, and lay down, grabbing the remote and turning the television on. She wanted and needed background noise.

But despite the Twilight Zone moments, she felt safer in this house than she'd felt for a while. She closed her eyes. A little nap wouldn't hurt, not at all.

15

Jasmine stood on a hill in a midnight dream world overlooking a windswept plain with stunted trees dotting the landscape. Shadows moved in the distances. Jasmine had experienced many nightmares, but only the waking ones were disturbing. She felt a cool wind on her face and leaned into it. She liked her dreams, no matter which way they twisted and turned. One thing was constant about dreams: they always ended.

She climbed down the hill, the huge, strange, silvery moon casting sharp shadows. Little creatures scampered out of her way. She reached the bottom and imagined herself sitting in one of the trees, and she was there, securely perched on a branch. That was the nice thing about dreams— the scenery changes.

The wind blew and the trees' tiny blue silver leaves shook and tinkled as if they were metallic. The dreamscape had a wild beauty, and she wished Raziq could share it with her. Jasmine ran her fingers through her hair. When he wasn't with her, which was seldom, she thought about him. He constantly invaded her dreams. Her breath quickened when she thought about how passionately her fantasies played out in the dream world.

He'd open his arms and she'd walk into them without a trace of fear, apprehension, or clothing. Ah yes, they were good in her dreams.

She blinked and the landscape changed. She stood in a place of hot winds and stony red cliffs under a blazing blue sky. Raziq soared through the air with Bless, heading toward her.

They'd almost reached her when Jasmine strangled a terrified scream. The skeletal demons she'd seen in New York appeared in the sky speeding toward her with blood-curdling yells, shooting black flames from their eyes. A flame hit her and she gasped with the pain of the burn. Screw this nightmare. Raziq was here, but no way were they getting to the good part soon. Besides, it hurt. Her lungs ached with the effort of her exertion and her shoulder still felt like it was on fire. . . . She wheeled and ran.

She stumbled and looked behind her. The creatures were almost upon her. Their fetid breath roiled in her nostrils. "Kill her," one said, its voice harsh and guttural, utterly nonhuman. Then fire exploded around her and she was blasted into the air. She fell lightly as if she were a feather, the burning remnants of the creatures dropping to the ground far more quickly.

She felt Raziq's arms around her as her feet settled to the earth.

His lips touched hers and she met his kiss greedily. His mouth opened, and his tongue delved sensuously, hungrily.

She twisted against his body, her fear forgotten in the wet heat of her arousal. "Ahem," a woman's voice said from behind. She twirled around, and Bless stood there, looking embarrassed.

"Why are you still in my dream?" Jasmine asked. "Usually about now that bed of clouds appears. I really like that bed."

"Bless and I are here, and we aren't asleep or dreaming. Our bodies are in the living room," Raziq said.

"I think we need to wake her," Bless said, scanning the horizon. "Usually they ignore dreamers, but she was directly attacked. They are watching for her. If she had been here alone, she probably would have been killed."

Nope, this dream was no fun at all, Jasmine decided.

Raziq looked grim. "We can't keep her from sleeping."

"But we can keep her out of the astral. Quick, I sense others approaching. You go; I'll stay and guard her until she wakes."

Raziq nodded and faded away.

"Awwwwww," Jasmine said. "You sent him away and he's always the highlight of my dreams."

"Pay attention; we don't have much time. Do you feel the energies around you, almost like the air? Try to sense them, concentrate and then draw them into your body as if you're inhaling."

Jasmine humored her and closed her eyes. She felt the air moving around her, pressing on her. It did feel as if she could pull it into her pores. The ground felt alive, the earth pulsing beneath her feet. For a moment it was as if she were a tree, her roots going deep into the earth, a part of it. But there was something else, something even more intimate that felt familiar and light. Fire. Fire that didn't burn, fire like air, water, earth, a part of her.

Jasmine stretched out her fingers and drew it in through her pores. It filled her body, tingling as if she'd become electrified.

She'd never felt so vital before. She opened her eyes and saw Bless beaming at her. She smiled back and opened her mouth to ask—

"Jasmine, wake up." Raziq's voice cut through her consciousness. She opened her eyes. He bent over her bed, peering into her eyes, his hands grasping her shoulders.

She inhaled his scent, and wished she were still dreaming.

Why couldn't she reach out and take what she wanted?

She was thirty-six years old and she deserved to have what she wanted, even if it was fattening, wicked, and she'd be bound to pay the price for indulging.

"Kiss me," she said, her breath rushing out.

His worry transformed to a smoldering gaze of sexual promise in an instant.

His lips touched hers, liquid fire. She raised her arms to pull him down to cover her, wanting his body deep inside her own.

"Raziq? Jasmine?" Bless called.

Raziq shut his eyes and visibly pulled himself together. "In here," he replied, his voice hoarse. He straightened and moved to a chair, sat, and crossed his legs.

Lord, she ached for him.

Bless entered the room, looking excited. "She drew the energies of fire, and in such a short time, too."

"Fire?" He looked pleased. "Another thing Jasmine and I have in common."

Jasmine felt as if she'd been punched in her gut. They were talking about *her* dream. As if, as if, they'd been present and it had really happened.

"You crossed over to the astral in your sleeping state," Raziq said. "Bless was training me, and you suddenly appeared. You were immediately attacked."

"And he destroyed an entire pack of demons with a single bolt," Bless added. "Impressive. I didn't have to lift a finger to help."

"There were no demons around until you arrived. We were looking for some. It was as if your presence drew them." Raziq darted a glance at Bless. "Is such a thing possible?"

Bless frowned and nodded. "This sorceress could have cast a spell on her that acted something like a homing device for demons."

"A friend of mine gave me a charm for her," Raziq said.

"Let's see it," Bless asked. They looked at Jasmine.

"Time the hell out," she said, holding her hands up in a T. "I'm still not past the part where you two end up in my dream." She pinched herself. "Am I still asleep?"

Bless crossed the room and sat beside Jasmine on the bed. "I know it's a lot to take in. But you need to accept the reality of the situation quickly. There's much danger."

"No shit, Sherlock," Jasmine knew she was being pissy, but her limit had been reached. "So you're telling me if I go to sleep, a horde of demons will be waiting to jump me?"

"Where is the charm?" Bless asked.

"I keep it in my suitcase."

Raziq frowned. "I told you to wear it. Was it in the luggage when the demon attacked?"

"It was. Sorry, Raziq, but I still hadn't really accepted the demon concept and that thing smells like ass. I didn't want to wear ass on my chest."

"If the choice goes down to smelling like ass or dying, I hope you're wise enough to choose to smell like ass," he growled.

"May I see the charm?" Bless asked again, with a sigh.

Jasmine pulled a suitcase on her bed, dug around, and pulled out a plastic bag.

Bless opened it and flinched.

"See, I told you it was funky," Jasmine said.

"I think I can make you a less odorous charm. This one is effective, but demonic; that's why the stink."

"Good. Raziq, don't worry. I'll wear it."

"I'll prepare a sleeping draught that will prevent you from crossing over to the astral. You must take it before you go to sleep. This house is well warded against demons, and I can take care of your car, but . . . ?"

"It's only a matter of time until one gets me," Jasmine finished.

"You can dig in, build a fortress, and ward it, as we have. Protect yourself."

"How do I live inside a fortress? I have to provide for myself," Jasmine said, protesting.

Bless shook her head. "I don't know. You've angered a powerful sorceress."

"*I* angered her," Raziq said. "And I will finish it. We will not spend our lives running. The sorceress is the tool the demons are using to hasten the end before the proper time."

Bless shuddered. "We won't have a chance without the Chosen. But how can you breach the protections that a person of her caliber and power uses? She's nearly invulnerable."

Jasmine sank back on the bed and buried her face in her hands. "If we don't do in the blond witchy woman, I'm toast," she said, her breath muffled. She wasn't close to worrying about Armageddon yet; the personal peril the demons threatened was bad enough.

Suddenly she had an idea.

"I know what we can do!" she said, lifting her head.

"What's that?" Raziq asked.

"We need to find another genie and make a wish. You said you all pool your common power to do about anything. You're human now—you get a wish."

"That's sort of simplistic," Bless said.

Raziq was nodding. "But it would probably work. I don't have to wish her dead, just stripped of power. But finding a djinni is easier said than done. There are few of us left. We don't know the physical locations of each other."

Rick came to the door holding the little girl. "I put Ricky down for his nap, and Glory wanted to give you a kiss before she lay down."

Bless gathered her child in her arms. "I'll put her to bed and then I'll start preparing the sleeping draughts and the charm. Whatever you're going to do, you need to do it quickly." She cocked her head and surveyed Jasmine. "If you need to search for something, consider seeking the aid of your spirits." With those words, she left the bedroom, by her husband's side.

"I wonder what she meant by contacting my spirits?"

"I don't know. We'll consult with her again once she gets her child into bed. But first—"

Raziq pulled her from the bed, folding her into him, and caught her mouth with his. Jasmine started to pull back in shock, but as the electricity of his firm mouth zipped through her, she leaned into him instead, wrapping her arms around his strong back, reveling in the feel of his mouth, the gentle probe of his tongue. She gave it up, gave him her all, her heart along with her body. Damn him.

He pulled away first, breathing hard, then started to pace, stopped, and pulled her back to him, caressing her cheek with his thumb. She couldn't take her eyes off his mouth or her attention off the hardness against her lower belly.

"I couldn't bear it if something happened to you," he said, his voice husky.

She pulled away, heart touched and disturbed. "Why couldn't you? We barely know each other. Once this sexual chemistry is satisfied—"

"Stop," he said, touching her lips. "Give us a chance."

"You have a chance, but why pretend this is some great love? Once we get what we've had building up between us for days out of our systems, you're free to move on."

"Why would I do that when the only place I want to be in the world is here with you?"

Why did he have to be so sweet like that? She reached out and rubbed the sexy stubble on his cheek. Lord help her, she was falling in love with this man, floating on washes of luscious chocolate cream by his side. She'd follow him anywhere, including hell. The downside was that it was looking like she might be there already.

"Let's go find Bless," she said. "We have demons to kill and a sorceress's spell to break."

He gave her a wry smile. "There's that, too."

Herbs were bubbling in a large pot on the stove, filling the air with fragrant steam.

"As secretary of state, Adrianne Dimontas will have more resources than magic and demons to search for her quarry," Bless said, handing Jasmine a vial of oil.

"I had a batch on hand," Bless said. "It's charmed to ward away demons and render you invisible to them. Put a tiny dab at the seven pulse points: the right side of your neck, both wrists, inside your left and right thighs, and the top of your feet."

Jasmine unscrewed the bottle and sniffed. "It smells like fish!"

"It's a degree better than smelling like ass," Bless said with a grin.

"Barely," Jasmine said.

"Fishy or not, you need to wear it always, and reapply it after you bathe. I need to find something for you to carry the sleeping draught in," Bless said, going through her cabinets. "There's a ziplock bag with pre-mixed herbs to make more, and I put the recipe in there, too."

"How do we consult the spirits to find djinn?" Raziq asked.

"I was going to give you several books that have the information you need. I feel you need to be on your way now, that what is supposed to have hap-

pened has passed, and you must hurry to whatever
the universe has in store for you next."

"We need to go west," Raziq said, nodding.

Jasmine's only inner urgings were to get laid,
and it didn't matter where it happened, particularly, as long as it happened soon.

Within a half hour they were at the car, ready to
go. Jasmine shook Rick's hand and then turned to
Bless. She impulsively threw her arms around her.
"Thank you for everything," she said. "You would
be a wonderful friend."

Bless's eyes twinkled. "I am your wonderful
friend," she said. "We'll see you two again soon."

The stars shone down as cold as ice. Jasmine
pulled out of the gates of the stone wall, feeling as
if she were leaving the last safe haven and venturing into the scary dark forest. She glanced over at
Raziq next to her. But things could be worse, after
all.

"Head west," Raziq said.

The feeling that she needed to complete something bordering on urgency struck her. That something was east and it had to do with setting things
straight. Something she had to do before she
moved on.

Raziq was studying a map by flashlight. She
pulled over.

"What's up?" he asked.

"I need to take a short detour east. Something I
have to do. I have to go to Macon. It's not far."

He drew in a quick breath. "I understand," he finally said. "You have to do what you need to do."

"Yeah." Jasmine made a U-turn and headed
back to her life that was.

An hour and a half later, she stood on the door-
step of the wife of her ex-lover. She'd become ac-

customed to the smell of the charmed oil, but she
prayed she would not smell fishy to the woman.
The woman she'd detested, the one she'd considered the single biggest obstacle to her happiness.
The woman from whom she'd stolen something
precious, the woman who she'd hurt again and
again without a second thought.

16

Jasmine rang the doorbell. "Get that, honey," she heard Keith's ex-wife call out.

A pretty girl, around ten years old, opened the door. Keith's daughter.

"May I speak to your mother? It's important."

The girl cocked her head, but made no move to go get her mother. "Jasmine. You selling something?" she asked, eyes intelligent and alert.

"I'm not selling anything. Go get your mother like I said."

Wariness filled the girl's face, but she backed away from the door. "All right," she said.

Sofia came out—a pretty brown-skinned woman with a slightly plump face and body. She was drying her hands on a dish towel. "Gretchen, go upstairs and take your brother with you."

Her daughter hesitated.

"Now!" Gretchen finally turned and ran from the room.

Sofia looked at Jasmine and raised her chin.

"What do you want?" Her voice was brittle with hostility.

"I want to tell you I'm sorry."

Sofia blinked. "Fine. You just did. Good-bye." She backed up, starting to push the door closed.

"Hold up," Jasmine said. "Now I know what I did to you. Me, not only Keith. I haven't suffered nearly enough."

"What do you want from me?" Sofia demanded. "Exoneration? Well, you ain't gonna get it here. You screwed my man for years, bitch."

"I was the fool, not you," Jasmine said. "I wanted to tell you that. He was wrong, too, but he had to have a fool to be wrong with. But, if it wasn't me, it would have been someone else. It wasn't about you. It wasn't your fault. No one woman could ever be enough for a dog like him."

Defensiveness drained out of Sofia's body, replaced by vulnerability. "No, I was the fool to put up with it for so long. A woman knows," she said, not meeting Jasmine's eyes.

Jasmine shook her head. "None of it was your fault. That's what I have to make you understand. You tried to hold your family together and hold the father of your children to his rightful place. Keith wasn't enough of a man for you. And . . . and I was never the woman you are. I can only hope that one day, God will forgive me and I can come close to measuring up to you."

Sofia's eyes widened.

Jasmine turned away, her eyes filling with tears. She walked down the porch stairs feeling the truth of every word she'd uttered. She was the fool and the coward, not Sofia, and while it hurt, somehow she felt lighter by finally acknowledging the fact instead of running away from it.

She climbed back into the driver's seat and wiped her eyes.

"Are you all right?" Raziq asked.

She nodded. "I'm ready to move on now."

"You look tired. We should stop."

"I can make it to Atlanta."

"I'm feeling we should still go to Salt Lake City."

"That's a hell of a drive. Believe me, we won't make it there tonight." Jasmine yawned, realizing she was exhausted, physically and emotionally. She was starving, too.

"Let's find a decent hotel and order in some food."

"It's been a long day."

She didn't bother to protest when Raziq got one room instead of two. She felt drained, empty, like tears had washed out her insides.

As soon as they got to the room, he tipped the bellhop and retrieved a thermos of the sleeping draught that Bless had made. "Drink this before you even sit down," he said, pouring a cupful into the lid. "I want to be close to you, just in case. I might be able to sense something and come when you need me."

Jasmine downed the draught and replaced the cup before she walked into his arms. He closed them around her and they stood for a space. He rocked her, a gentle motion that soothed her. "I want to be close to you, too. But not tonight. Tonight I need to—"

He touched her lip with a finger and traced its outline. "You need to rest."

"But I don't want to let you go," she said.

"You won't have to. Don't you realize by now that I'm going to hold you and not let you go?"

He was true to his word. He ordered from room

service while she showered. Jasmine was able to down only a few bites before she crawled into bed.

A few minutes later, she heard the shower running and soon, there he was next to her, pulling her tenderly against him, spooning her in his grasp. She exhaled in satisfaction.

It wasn't about his being fine or that tremendous bulge in his trousers. It was about the man he was—his kindness, humor, gentleness, and intelligence all wound up with this aura of imperturbable power. It felt as if she knew him down to the core of his soul, the good and the bad both, and all this was a part of her, too.

Something gave within her, and she wanted to gasp with the sharp pain of it. She let it sweep through her, exposing her being as if she stood in front of a searchlight and cleansing the dirty corners of her soul.

It was still night when Jasmine woke with Raziq's lips two inches away. Yellowed street light mixed with the silver of the full moon shone through the pulled curtains. His long lashes lay against his cheeks, as innocent as a boy's. That was the only thing boyish about him.

His face was all planes and jutting angles, shadowed with masculine stubble. There was something noble and wild about it, not a modern man. She could picture him with Hannibal's armies fighting off the Romans. He was in the world then, alive and well, his origins going back before the ascent of man—she couldn't imagine knowing the depths of him, the knowledge and experience he must have.

His chest rose and fell. His breath smelled of smoke.

She touched her lips against his, firm, warm, *responsive*. In a swift movement, he rolled over, his body pressing hers into the mattress.

"I've wanted you forever," he said, his voice sleep-drenched.

Her heart pounded as his mouth descended, achingly slowly. Then, finally, her lips softened under the onslaught of his hungry kiss.

He raised his head and Jasmine saw her blaze of rising passion mirrored in his eyes.

"I want you, too," she said.

He rolled his hips against her, the hardness of his erection making her gasp and her legs open, needing. "There's no stopping this time," he said, with a hint of the harshness of his need.

Jasmine reached for his lips again, her legs wrapping around his hips. She met the thrust of his tongue eagerly. He pulled her ass tight against him with one hand, and the other pushed up her T-shirt. She helped him draw it over her head.

His eyes trailed fire against her breasts and he took a hard nipple into his mouth and sucked, then the other. She cried out, the feel of his mouth on her breasts searing. She tangled her fingers in his crisp curls, wanting more of him. She pressed her groin against his erection, a long, slow grind, a surge of hot liquid sex. She had to have him inside her. She grasped his T-shirt in greedy fists.

He moaned, and his hand went to her panties, pulling down the thin bit of lace and silk.

He sat up and pulled away his T-shirt and briefs. It seemed as if a flicker of fire emanated from his body, something like a halo.

His erect penis was full, rock hard, and high. It was a beautiful thing. She cupped him with one hand and grasped his shaft with the other. She twirled her tongue around the head and he moaned.

"Baby, I'm not going to last ten seconds like that," he said, panting.

"Give it to me then," she whispered.

He tumbled her back on the bed, and his fingers parted her moist curls as she pushed against him, hips writhing, seeking.

She reached for him with both hands blindly, her thumbs whirling beads of liquid around his swollen head.

Raziq gave an animal groan and pushed against her opening, trying to enter her in a single deep thrust.

Her body tightened, her hands raking into his back.

He held back, teeth gritting, "I have to give it to you baby. Take me in."

"Ohhh, you're so . . . it hurts, Raz."

"Quiet, baby. We'll take it slow. Relax for me, and take it, baby, take it a bit at a time."

He eased in. She moaned, not in pain but in pleasure, tightening around him, drawing him in.

"Oh baby, you're so tight. So good."

She wanted more. She tilted her hips, pressing his tight rear to accept him all. He started to move in earnest, rolling his hips, filling her with all of him.

He plunged against her, pinning her hips against the bed with each stroke.

She strained back, meeting him stroke for stroke, feeling his fullness against her walls as something like heaven. But there was more urgency than she'd ever felt before.

She wrapped her legs higher around his hips,

pulling him still deeper, stretching her more, hitting sweet spot. Flames whipped into to a raging inferno, driving out thought, humanity, anything but—

Explosion. Oh God, she shattered into nova, blinding starshine, spasming into blackness and exploding into blindness again, stealing her breath and . . . and . . .

Then he was slamming into her, gasping his own completion.

They subsided in each other's arms, sweaty and satiated.

Jasmine squeezed her eyes shut, but still tears leaked down her cheeks.

Raziq drew a sharp breath. "I hurt you. Why didn't you say something? Damn, I'm sorry, baby."

He looked as if he were going to cry himself.

She touched his cheek. "No, no, you didn't hurt me at all." She exhaled. "That was my first time, that's all."

He looked surprised.

"No, I'm not a virgin. That would be a joke. But it was my first time with a man inside me, you know. I—I used to think that something was wrong with me that I couldn't finish the way, the way I supposed other women did."

He kissed her so tenderly that something in her heart gave way. "Baby, that might have been your first, but I promise it won't be your last."

The next morning when she and Raziq loaded the SUV, she noticed that the atmosphere had changed between them. She hadn't noticed the level of tension that had existed between them previously until it was gone.

She pulled onto I-75 and Raziq opened one of the tomes that Bless had given him. "Tonight, I'm going to try to summon spirits and find out what we need to know."

Unease roiled within her. The thought of doing such a thing went against her deepest grain. It was worse now that she believed that spirits were real.

"I don't want to summon spirits," she said.

He glanced at her. "Fine, you can stay out of the room. This car is well warded."

"I don't want you to do it, either."

"We don't have much time. We have to find a djinni and quickly. Don't worry, spirits can't harm the living."

"Raziq, it seems wrong, tainted somehow. Is there any other way?"

He hesitated and then shook his head. "I'm sorry, but no, there's no other way to quickly find out what we need to know."

Hours later past Atlanta, into Tennessee, twilight purpled into night. Jasmine insisted on driving all day, gaining some satisfaction from burning up highway miles under her tires. She wished she could drive all night, all day and all night again, drive right to their solution with no other detours.

"Take the next exit," Raziq directed.

"There's no motel off that exit, no services at all. A few more miles down the road . . ."

"That's the exit we need to take," he said. "I want to do the ritual around here."

"Now?" Jasmine's voice came out in a croak. "I thought we were going to do it in a hotel room."

"It's safer out here. The car is warded and won't allow the entry of any stray spirit. It's safer in the open."

She swallowed hard and pulled off the exit.

"Get off the main road as soon as you can. We want an open field without a lot of traffic driving by."

The country highway was lit only by a bright moon. She pulled onto a gravel road with a dark, abandoned farmhouse.

"I'll drive past the farmhouse. It seems quiet here." Raziq caressed her cheek.

"Don't be afraid," he said.

"We gotta do what we gotta do," she said.

She parked in a clearing within sight of the farmhouse.

"I won't be long," Raziq said.

"I'm coming with you."

"You'll be safe in the car."

"I know, but we're in this together. All the way."

He stared her a moment, then with a swift movement pulled her to him and touched her lips with his, a promise.

17

He rummaged through the trunk, pulling out a bundle wrapped in white silk. "Could you bring the two books on the top of the pile in the front seat?" he asked.

She retrieved the books and he unwrapped the silk, unfolding it out in a neat square on the grass. He placed four indistinguishable objects at each of the four corners. Then he placed a bowl, a mirror, and a silk bag in the middle. He grasped a dagger and stood.

"What do you want me to do?" Jasmine asked.

"Sit there and don't move, no matter what happens. Hold the flashlight on the book." Jasmine nodded, shivering.

Raziq raised the dagger, point toward the sky. He opened a book, but barely glanced at it as he made gestures with the dagger and uttered phrases in a strange tongue. He finished with a flourish and said, "That was the banishing ritual. Now comes the real deal. I'm going to call on your guardian spirits for info."

"I have guardian spirits?" jasmine asked.

"Bless assured me that you do."

"What if I had stayed in the car, Raziq?"

He grinned, looking wolflike in the moonlight. "I knew you were too much of a woman to cower in the car when there was action going on."

She wanted to hit him.

"So this entire endeavor depends on the good-will of my guardian angels?"

"Spirits. Angels are a different thing, but not entirely. I'm going to put a general call to any informed parties also, in case they happen to be in the neighborhood."

Jasmine looked around her, the pristine clearing lit by the glowing half moon, the trees in the near distance, the low stones scattered about. "Raziq?"

"What?"

"You may have more spirits than you bargained for."

"Why's that?"

"We're sitting in the middle of a graveyard."

He looked around and shrugged. "It's an old graveyard. There are no fresh graves. Any lingering spirits attached to their decaying human bodies are long gone."

"Somehow I'm not reassured."

"I completed the banishing ritual. It's all right. The purpose was to rid the environs of negative influences." He opened the silken bag and sprinkled some dark substance into the bowl, pulled a cigarette lighter from his pocket, and set it alight.

"Try to clear your mind of fear, anxiety, and dread. Concentrate on your breath, watch the mirror, and illuminate the book for me."

Jasmine took a deep breath and recrossed her legs. She stared at the mirror and tried to concentrate on her breathing. That didn't work. She shifted her attention to Raziq's lips. Much better.

He sat on the ground across from her and chanted from the book as fragrant smoke drifted from the bowl between them, wafting to the sky in the still, chill air. His voice was deep and soothing, almost hypnotizing.

Long, long moments passed. Her ass was cold and her legs were cramping. This wasn't working. Raziq was going to be hoarse as hell in the morning.

And still he chanted, his eyes half-closed.

Then she heard a buzz, as if distant electricity were gathering. "Watch the mirror," Raziq whispered in English among the torrent of babble that poured from his throat. "They've crossed the veil. They're here."

Jasmine gazed at the mirror in horror as the smoke seemed to gather within it. The glass appeared to inhale and exhale.

Raziq picked up the knife and drew it across his wrist. Jasmine gasped as a drop of dark blood splashed across the mirror.

The mirror absorbed it. She fell backward, her hands on the cold earth, prepared to scramble away.

"I want to find one who is of the blood I once shared—a true djinni."

"You're on the right path."

Jasmine's cold fingers touched her lips. The voice was her mother's. She stumbled to the mirror, hand outstretched.

"Don't touch it!" Raziq said sharply.

She pulled back her hand. "Was that my mother?" she asked, hearing the whimper in her voice.

"I don't know. I need you to concentrate. Clear your mind." He resumed chanting.

A wind rose up around them, full of spirit whispers. Jasmine trembled with more than cold.

A chorus of ghostly whispers emerged from the mirror. "Listen, listen for the path," the spirits whispered.

Raziq drew a pad and pen from his jacket pocket.

"By the silver river and rosy rock
The ley line runs with it
To awaken the fire within,
Or the salt of the earth
Is blasted by a silver wind
And evil triumphs, victorious."

The voices faded away.

Jasmine wiped her face with her sleeve. Her face was covered with cold tears and her nose was running. She doubted she'd ever be calm again.

Then Raziq's warm arms were gathering her into his hard chest. She shivered against him for a space, and he rocked her back and forth gently, whispering soothing words. She closed her eyes and inhaled his smoky scent. And in that space she knew without a doubt that if he could protect her, he would.

She raised her head. "Let's go. We'll try again another time."

"There's no need. We have the information we need."

"It sounded vague to the point of nonsensical to me."

"Oh, they always do that," he said. "It's a spirit thing. It's very annoying. But the info is there. We only have to figure it out."

"Oh."

"I need to do another banishing ritual," he said.

She watched him as he moved with the dagger, warmth curling through her belly. Such a beautiful man, and for the moment all hers.

As soon as they got into the car, he drew her into his arms, his mouth touching, tasting, licking hers. Ah, she wanted him so.

But—"Let's get out of this graveyard," she said, starting the car.

He settled back into the seat with a sigh. "True, we have all night ahead of us."

Jasmine drove down the highway, alert and awake.

"There are plenty of hotels in Nashville," Raziq said.

"I want to get clear of the city," she said.

You're on the right path. Had that been her mother's voice? Maybe she wished it so, a semihallucination brought on by stress. *You're on the right path.* She prayed that it was so, and most of all, she hoped it was her mother who was letting her know.

She glanced over. Raziq was asleep, head lolling back against the headrest. She felt guilty. He would be in a warm, clean bed if she had stopped when he'd asked.

The next exit said there was lodging. She pulled into a small, seedy hotel. Raziq stirred but didn't wake as she got out of the car.

She rang the bell for the night clerk. Minutes passed and she rang again. Just as she turned back to the car, the lights to the office went on and a glamorous blond woman, looking as if she had just stepped out of the beauty salon, opened the door.

"We need a room," Jasmine said.

"That's what we do and we aim to please." The

woman opened a cabinet behind her and studied the keys. "Here's a nice one. One seventeen." She handed Jasmine the key.

"Don't you want to know what type of room we want?"

"Oh, yeah. What type of room do you want?"

"What do you have available?"

"Room one seventeen," the woman answered.

Jasmine sighed. "All right. How much is it?"

"Um. Ten dollars."

"That's mighty cheap."

"That's because we only take cash."

Jasmine figured the woman was running some sort of game, but this was a national chain. She was probably the manager's daughter—or girlfriend wanting cigarette money.

A wave of sudden fatigue washed over her. Whatever. They only needed the room for the night, anyway, and she didn't feel as if she could drive another mile.

She opened her purse and dug in it for the ten dollars. She handed the money over and the woman pressed the key in her hand. "Sleep well," she said.

Room one seventeen was in the back. Jasmine parked by the door. "Raziq, wake up," she said, nudging him.

"Where are we?" he asked.

"Some motel. I'm too tired to help bring in the luggage. I'm just going to grab my cosmetic case and get the rest in the morning."

"I'll get your bag," Raziq said.

"Thanks." She opened the room and flipped on the light. It was spacious and surprisingly clean and modern, with two queen-size beds. For ten dollars it looked like she had hit pay dirt.

She yawned and dropped her clothes on the

chair nearest the bed and crawled under the covers in her underwear. She didn't think she could keep her eyes open another moment.

She'd just closed her eyes when Raziq was shaking her awake. "You forgot to take your draught." He sounded stern and upset as he proffered the full thermos cap to her. "You can't forget, Jasmine. Your life depends on it."

She swallowed the nasty stuff in a gulp and curled back under the covers.

The next thing Jasmine heard was Raziq's irritated whisper. "What the hell are you doing here, Susie?"

"What sort of welcome is that for an old friend?" a woman purred.

"We were never that tight. And you know things are different now."

"And how," the woman said.

"Keep your hands off my dick, dammit."

"I always thought you looked hot, but now that you're human, I bet you feel mighty hot, too."

"Begone, demon," Raziq grumbled.

"Asshole."

"C'mon, Susie, you're going to wake up Jasmine."

"And what of it? Anyway, I know an incubus who'd be just her type."

"Do it and I'll send your ass back to hell so fast you won't know what hit you."

"Oooh, so manly."

"Give it a break."

Jasmine sat up, deciding she wasn't dreaming after all. She gasped as she spied the blond woman who had given her the key to the room, wearing see-through pink baby doll pajamas, reclining on the bed with Raziq. The blonde was extraordinarily well endowed. Her boobs looked like torpedos ready to launch.

Raziq was sitting ramrod straight against the headboard, looking exasperated.

The woman waggled her fingers at Jasmine. "See you later, big boy," she said to Raziq and dissipated in a puff of smoke.

Jasmine let out a squeaky scream.

Raziq sniffed. "Succubi get on my damn nerves," he said.

"What the hell is going on here?" Jasmine demanded.

"Susie is a succubus, a female demon. They like to have sex with human men. Sometimes they kill them, but not always. Susie is pretty harmless. Basically, she likes to have sex."

"And how do you know her?" Jasmine asked, her jaw clenched and her muscles tensing.

"We go back."

"What's up? What do you mean you go back?" Jasmine knew her voice rose on the last few words, but she couldn't help it. Raziq looked nervous.

"Seven millennia stuck in a bottle can get a little boring. Occasionally when I was out, I'd get together with some other benign magical beings, maybe Trent, or a few other hybrids, some incubi and a succubus or two."

"Y'all had weird sex parties?" Jasmine asked, not knowing whether to be revolted or titillated.

"Not weird and no sex, either. Remember that little interspecies problem? And succubi and incubi want to do it only with humans."

"I know that's right, honey," a disembodied voice said.

Jasmine jumped straight up. "That's it!" she yelled.

"Susie, get out of here!" Raziq yelled. "I'm not playing."

She materialized, draped over a chair, totally nude. "Or what are you gonna do? Fuck me?"

Jasmine was pulling on her clothes. "We're leaving," she said.

"Susie's harmless," Raziq said.

"I don't care. We need to bounce."

"Jasmine . . ."

She raised her hand. "You can stay if you want to, but I'm out of here, with or without you."

"We can go, not a problem. But there's no need to rush—"

Jasmine sniffed.

"Emotional, isn't she?" Susie said.

"Out!" Raziq roared.

"Okay." The succubus raised perfectly manicured hands. "Keep your pants on. Or as I prefer, not." She smoked out, trailing trills of laughter and obnoxious fumes of Giorgio perfume.

Jasmine left her blouse half-buttoned and grabbed the keys. She got in the car, slamming the car door shut behind her. She saw Raziq following with a bag and she popped the back door for him. Sticking the keys in the ignition, she had the urge to drive away and leave him.

She knew from somewhere outside herself that she was overreacting. It felt as if she'd been waiting for the other shoe to drop and *boom*, there it was.

Raziq got into the car and fastened his seat belt. "The car is warded. Susie can't invade here," he said.

"How did she find you?"

He shrugged. "Maybe when I summoned the spirits. That sort of magic opens you. She might have been close and heard my call and recognized it."

"Can we ward the hotel rooms?" she asked.

"No," he said.

"That's not acceptable."

He shifted in his seat. "Jasmine, I'm tired. What I was trying to say is that Susie is harmless—and I prefer to go to sleep in a real bed if I can. So do you."

Jasmine bit her lip, trying to trust him, trying to suppress her insecurities. "I'll stop when we get closer to St. Louis."

Many miles later, they checked into a Ramada. She asked for a single room. She'd share a bed with Raziq. The next time a succubus climbed into his bed, she wanted to know about it ASAP.

They fell exhausted into the bed as soon as they got into the room. Raziq mumbled that he'd bring in their bags tomorrow.

When Jasmine woke the next morning, her mouth felt like cotton, and her eyes were gluey. She saw that her bags were stacked neatly close to her bed. Thank the Lord, Raziq had awakened early and brought them in. She heard the shower running and peered at the red numerals of the digital clock next to the bed. A quarter after ten. She'd overslept.

She heard the jangle of keys in the door. It must be the maid. Jasmine pulled the covers up to her chin and rose up on an elbow, intending to call out and ask her to return later. But a beautiful Hispanic woman walked into the room before she could get the words out. The woman wore a skimpy maid's costume, the skirt barely covering her butt. Jasmine frowned as she smelled Giorgio perfume.

The maid closed the door. "I just thought I'd take care of Raziq's morning hard-on for you, honey," she said. Jasmine's jaw dropped as the maid stepped out of her clothes and left them puddled on the floor. She sashayed bare-ass naked into the bathroom where Raziq showered.

18

"Oh no, you don't," Raziq heard Jasmine yell. "The only one who's going take care of my man's erection is me!"

"Says who?" another feminine voice said belligerently.

Susie. Oh, hell. Raziq turned off the water, snatched a towel, wrapped it around his waist, flung aside the shower curtain, and stepped out.

He sucked air through his teeth when he saw that Jasmine had Susie in a headlock. Jasmine had on a lacy demibra and thong; Susie, in the guise of a long haired bronze beauty, was stark naked. He blinked rapidly at the image. God, they looked hot together.

"Susie, what are you doing here? Jasmine, let her go."

"After I kick her demon ass back to hell," Jasmine said, teeth bared.

Susie sniffed. "What's that? Fish?" She raised a brow in Jasmine's direction. "It seems as if you need a shower, honey."

Susie's head snapped to the side as the sound of Jasmine's slap rang through the small bathroom.

Susie grabbed her cheek. "That hurt. Are you going to let her slap me around, Raziq? We go way back."

"Let her go, Jasmine," Raziq said.

"You know that I have to wear the charmed oil!" Jasmine said. "The bitch said I smell like fi—"

"Now!" he roared.

"Fine. I'm gone." Jasmine wheeled and stalked off.

Oh, shit, through the door he could see Jasmine pulling on her jeans. "Will you calm down?" he asked. "You know I don't want Susie like that, girl. No way. But I told you she's harmless. She's a creature of base instinct and hitting her isn't going to make her go away."

"Then what is gonna make her go away?"

At just the wrong time, Susie snuck up behind him and her hand snaked under his towel. He yelped in surprise.

"Oh, no, you don't," Jasmine yelled again and charged. She caught Susie in an impressive linebacker's tackle and they both went sailing toward the bed and landed hard. There was a crack and the mattress hit the floor.

Then Jasmine got busy trying to wring Susie's neck. Susie turned an interesting shade of purple.

Raziq sighed and reached for his jeans. It wasn't like Jasmine could kill Susie or anything, but she sure was aggressive. His face heated as he realized how sexy he was finding the entire scene.

"I'm not averse to a threesome," Susie's disembodied voice said from the vicinity of the ceiling.

Jasmine yelped in surprise and fell over, releasing the succubus.

"Or maybe Raziq would prefer to watch us?" Susie sat up, rubbing her neck. She eyed Raziq's bulge. "Yeah, I bet he'd like that, all right."

"Get out, Susie, and I'm not telling you again," Raziq said.

"But—"

"I mean it!" Raziq's voice thundered.

She pouted and faded out.

"And what in God's name got into you?" Raziq rounded on Jasmine.

She studied her nails. "That bitch pissed me off."

He had never wanted to spank a woman so badly. "How old are you? Fifteen?"

Jasmine rolled off the bed. "I'm taking a shower."

He heard the water running, and he started a pot of coffee in the too-little coffee maker. He had no idea what had gotten into Jasmine, but he had to admit that the sight of naked Susie and barely clad Jasmine was the hottest thing he'd encountered in his djinni or human life. He wished he could have gotten it on film. Gods!

And she was taking a shower. Naked. The thought drew him into the bathroom. He watched her through the hazy glass of the shower door. Jasmine had her face buried in the washcloth, obviously sobbing.

He let his jeans drop to the floor and got under the spray with her, drawing her into his arms. He wanted to protect her from harm, from any pain. He wished he could make her understand that Susie was no threat, the most minor of demons and wholly unappealing to him.

He knew Susie, her real self and her real appearance. Her different human guises were only costumes to him. Demons never had turned him on.

Jasmine relaxed against him, then stiffened. "I bet she's watching."

"Who cares if she is?" he said.

"I do. Why don't you get dressed? I'll be out in a bit." Her voice was colder than the water.

He'd get her to understand. Susie was mighty small stuff compared to what they were facing.

"Fine, baby. I'll be waiting for you."

The next day, they drove for hours in silence. Raziq immersed himself in the books Bless had given him. Bless had told him that she'd developed the power to kill the demons directly without crossing into the astral. She'd said that she'd transformed a physical knife into astral form and used it to kill demons.

Now, if she sensed a demon, she could instantly transform a lethal object into its astral form and kill the unseen demon, projected with her will.

Time was running out.

He shone the flashlight on the spirit words.

By the silver river and rosy rock
The ley line runs with it
To awaken the fire within,
Or the salt of the earth
Is blasted by a silver wind
And evil triumphs, victorious.

The fire within must have to do with him, an exdjinni. A dormant power. But how to awaken it? And most of all, how to use it?

The words blurred before his eyes. Jasmine was a trooper, driving for hours, playing that same Janis Joplin CD over and over. When he found the djinni, he was going to be hard pressed not to wish never to hear Janis Joplin again.

"We need to stop soon," he said.

"I was thinking about stopping for something more to eat in Denver, but decided to drive on through so we'd miss the worst traffic."

"I was referring to stopping for the night," Raziq said.

"Okay. I'm not very tired, though. Too much coffee, I guess." Jasmine was silent for a moment. "I wonder what guise that bitch succubus is going to importune you with tonight?" she mused.

He shrugged. "As long as she doesn't wake me up doing it, I don't really give a damn."

Jasmine drew in a sharp breath. "You want her to importune you!"

"You're being ridiculous. You need to calm down and quit it."

She banged her hands on the steering wheel in temper. "I'm pulling over right now. I'm getting out! No, screw that. You're the one getting out. Get out right now! You can wait for your honey on the side of the road."

There were some areas where humans lost their rationality at intervals. Jasmine apparently had chosen to lose her mind over Susie. Her irrational hate would have been far better directed toward the sorceress. But he had never claimed to understand the hows and whys of women all that well. They were all the same, whatever variety, and some things didn't change. A dim memory told him it was best to go with the flow as far as women and their idiosyncrasies were concerned.

"I'll do a spell and get rid of Susie," he said.

She darted a glance at him and her hands tightened on the wheel. "Really? How?"

"I read an incantation in one of the books that I might be able to modify."

Jasmine's fingers relaxed on the wheel. "As long as it works. I guess I'll stop at the next decent hotel. I've been driving for ages."

Raziq opened the silk square and yawned. "This is a summoning spell, to summon protective spirits," he said.

"Do you need me to do something to help you with the spell?" she asked.

"I'm all right." He wasn't, though. He was exhausted and couldn't wait to get this over with. He didn't understand how Jasmine looked so fresh and awake after hours of driving, while he, the passenger, felt drained.

Raziq spread the white silk cloth on the bed and laid out the implements. He did the summoning spell, lit the bowl of powdered incense, and then cleared his mind to chant the precise words of the ritual.

His eyes closed as he drifted into a half-sleep state, the words flowing from his tongue.

Warm breasts pressed into his back. He twisted his neck and looked into Jasmine's warm brown eyes. But he sensed something wasn't quite right.

There was no time to react as he spied a red globe over Jasmine's shoulder. He opened his mouth to yell and his body instinctively moved to cover Jasmine's.

But it was too late. Adrianne Dimontas appeared with a triumphant smile, raised her wand, and blasted Jasmine into a fine spray of hamburger meat and red bloody mist.

The mirror cracked and broke, and Dimontas screamed in terror as shadows streamed out of the mirror toward her. The sorceress shimmered and disappeared. Raziq stared at his hands, covered with the blood and flesh of the woman he loved.

"What happened?" Jasmine cried, rushing out of the bathroom.

19

Raziq stared at Jasmine in disbelief, speechless.

"Where did you come from?" he managed to get out.

"I had to go to the bathroom, sorry. This room looks like a slaughter pit," she said. "That's some gory spell you're casting."

Jasmine screamed as the room shimmered and the blood and gore slowly coalesced into human form. Her exact double stood beside Raziq, its hands clasped to the sides of its face as if it were trying to hold its head together.

"Damn, that hurt," Susie said. "Shit, Raziq, who was that blond bitch who blasted me to smithereens? How many women do you have, anyway?"

"You better watch out for that blonde," Susie said to Jasmine. "She packs one hell of a punch. Raziq, I was going to hang around for a while and treat you to that threesome you were dying for, but your blond bitch is scary, not to mention painful. I'm outta here. Try not to be too upset, okay?" Susie shimmered out with a grimace.

"We have to leave," Raziq said, galvanized into action. "She'll be back."

"Susie?" Jasmine asked. She was numb with what she'd witnessed. The significance of all the blood and gore sank in.

"The sorceress. The spirits chased her off. She thinks she killed you. But she'll be back for me."

He grabbed the car keys and pressed them into Jasmine's hands.

"But our luggage—" she said.

"Can be replaced. Let's go."

She thought about the bits of flesh and spray of blood that had flecked the walls. She grabbed her purse and they both headed for the car at a run.

"How did she find us?" Jasmine asked, foot on the gas.

"Slow down. We can't afford to be pulled over." Raziq massaged his throbbing temple. "It must have been the spell. Something went wrong. Somehow I alerted the demons to our presence—again. Thank the gods Susie showed up when she did."

"Susie," Jasmine said, her voice dripping disgust.

"She saved your life," Raziq said. "If that had been you . . ." He shuddered.

"True. Once I'm shredded into little bits and pieces, I stay shredded."

"I don't see how you can joke about it," Raziq said.

"What else can I do? I think you need to lay off the spells."

"I'm inclined to agree."

"I was tired after all when we stopped. I'm not going to be able to drive all night," Jasmine said.

"We'll park and sleep in the car. But first, we need to put some distance between—"

"I totally agree."

Jasmine drove a little over the speed limit but not too fast to draw the attention of the law.

They stopped at a small-town Super Wal-Mart that was open twenty-four hours to stock up on clothing, supplies, and food. Jasmine frowned at the amount of rugged camping supplies Raziq bought: tent, sleeping bags, cooking equipment, the works. And he bought food in bulk: bottles of vitamins, grains, beans, jerky, and dried fruit. He bought enough stuff to camp out for a year.

She'd never been the outdoor type, but it looked as if she was going to learn. "Where are we going?" she asked, after they had finally finished loading up the SUV and tying the tarpaulin across the supplies fitted into the roof top luggage rack. "We can't run forever."

A shadow crossed his face. "No, we can't.

She leaned against the car, bone weary. "What are we going to do? You know that nothing makes sense to me any more. I need you to talk to me."

"All right," Raziq said, not meeting her eyes. "Let's get started first, though."

As they pulled out of the parking lot, he said, "I want to start driving."

She glanced at him. "Death wish? What makes you think I want to die with you?"

He snorted with laughter. "I can start practicing on country roads in the mornings, at least."

"Are you trying to change the subject? You still need to talk to me about what's happening to us."

"Maybe I was. There's not a lot to say. I have this urge, indefinite but strong, that we need to head west, toward the mountains, toward Utah as fast as we can. It feels as if we are to be outdoors, somewhere away from people and habitation."

Jasmine frowned. "For how long? Do you expect us to skulk indefinitely in the Utah wilderness? It's cold outside. This is not my style at all."

"Everything will be all right."

"Are you sure about that?"

The silence was too long.

"Raziq?"

She darted a glance over at him. He rubbed his head as if a headache threatened to break out.

"The spirits said to awaken the fires within—or evil would win . . . so I guess I have to figure out some way to manipulate fire on this plane, the same as I can in the astral. But I've tried everything and I'm at a loss. Since I have the strong urge to go to the wilderness, I can only hope the gods are planning to enlighten me there."

"When you were a genie, you used fire to stop the sorceress until you could get us into the . . ."

"Diet Coke can."

"Yeah. Isn't the sorceress human?"

"The demons call magic practitioners 'tools,' but yes, she's human."

"She shot enough energy through her wand to blast Susie to particles. So how'd she do that?"

He frowned. "I assumed she worked a spell and accomplished her ends through demonic power. That's how they usually do that sort of thing." A thoughtful look crossed his face. "But her powers do seem far too impressive for mere magic and borrowed demonic energies."

"Is it possible that different people have different powers? Bless has true dreams; maybe some people read minds or bend spoons. Your power may be to start fires."

A look of frustration crossed Raziq's face. "I can't light a match. Believe me, I tried," he said.

"Did we come this far to fail?" Jasmine asked.

Raziqs lips thinned. "No. No, I promise you that we didn't."

"Well, we won't, then. We will find some way to stop the sorceress, demons be damned."

Raziq cocked his head and considered her. "You're a hell of a woman, do you know that?"

Jasmine said nothing, because she felt all too human.

She pulled into a rest area and parked close to the eighteen-wheelers. They folded down the seats and unfolded their sleeping bags, finally settling down to rest. Raziq pulled her into his arms and she moved closer to him, feeling his lips move in her hair.

"The universe can't take you from me. I'm used to you in this human life. Promise me," he said.

She closed her eyes, pain and pleasure mingled. "I won't leave you, Raziq." She wouldn't. But she knew in her heart that it was only a matter of time until he left her. That was what she deserved. No more, and no less.

He kissed her, tenderly and gently, building to a slow, seeking kiss that made her moan with desire. "Let me pleasure you," he said, his hands moving to unbutton, loosen, and remove.

His eyes seemed to feast on her exposed flesh in the dim light glowing with barely banked fires. "You are incredibly beautiful."

Jasmine had never considered her belly button an erotic spot. Her abdominal muscle clenched and her hips rotated with desire. "Raziq," she whispered.

Her breath rushed in with a sharp gasp as his cool tongue parted her lower lips.

Oh God. She was past thought, past anything but

sensation. It was like a lava flow building, building, edging to the crest, oh Lord, faster, no, no, no, don't stop. And the mountaintop exploded in flames.

She came together slowly, her breath harsh and panting.

He tore at his own clothes. He entered her slowly; she felt his tension, holding back, trying not to hurt her. She tipped her hips to take him in and wrapped her legs around his waist. He filled her up so good.

He moved, igniting a new fire within her, matching her slowly rising passion.

Wondrous. Tempo quickening. Beating against one another, wet and heavy with passion. Tumbling together toward . . . oh yes, again, almost.

He cried out, stiffening and flooding her with wetness. His passion within her pushed her over the edge and she spasmed around him, the feeling so strong that she shouted for the first time in her life. His name on her lips, fingers digging into his shoulders, her body claiming this man for her own. Again and again, waves of pleasure crashed, rushing her away. Burying her face in Raziq's neck, she inhaled his scent, and bit back a sob. She was floundering in the wide sea, this man her only anchor. Lost.

The next day lengthened into long, weary hours. They left the plains behind and entered the foothills of rugged mountains. Raziq steered her away from major highways. She traveled two-lane highways through small towns and hamlets, the air wintry; the road was no longer dotted with fast-food places and rest stops every few miles. The countryside was dark and rugged, guarded by craggy mountains. Wilderness.

"I'm getting tired."

"Pull off the road and let me drive," Raziq said.

"You've had only the one practice session," she said. "And it's getting dark."

"It wasn't as hard as I thought. Don't you feel the need to press on? Pull over for a moment. I want you to try something."

Jasmine pulled onto the shoulder of the road.

"Close your eyes and try not to think. Concentrate on your breath, the way Bless showed you. Try to notice one thing only, how you feel right here." He touched her abdomen.

His voice was low and compelling. She closed her eyes, breathed, and hoped she didn't fall asleep. Then she tried not to think about falling asleep, which made her think about it more.

Then she became aware of a pressure inside her gut where Raziq had pressed. A gnawing. It was anxious, maybe even urgent. There was something she had to do, somewhere she was supposed to be. It felt as if she had an urgent engagement, something like an interview for a job she really, really wanted, and if she didn't hurry, she'd be late.

"Okay, drive," Jasmine said. "I'll nap, but I'd like to wake safe and sound, if you don't mind."

"You felt it, didn't you?" he asked, a broad grin spreading across his handsome face.

She said nothing. Of course she was anxious; who wouldn't be?

He opened his door to get out. "Get some rest. You'll be fine," he said.

20

Jasmine opened her eyes. They were parked in a grove of trees, with no road in sight. She couldn't believe she'd slept through Raziq's driving off the road.

He'd lowered the driver's seat and he lay on his side, his breathing deep and regular. Long lashes fanned against his cheeks, the chiseled, masculine planes of his face offsetting his momentary vulnerability. A wash of emotion flowed through Jasmine. She might as well admit to herself how much she loved this man. She felt as if she needed him as much as she needed air.

But love was the enemy.

The thought reminded Jasmine of how frustrated she had felt by her best friend's struggle with food. Jasmine liked to eat, but Carmel loved food. Carmel loved preparing it, savoring new flavors and textures.

Carmel had overcome overeating. She was still a big girl, but undeniably healthy. Toned, her body was curvy, taut, and voluptuous. Carmel didn't overeat, but rather ate well. It baffled Jasmine when Carmel referred to food as the enemy.

But now Jasmine understood the war that went with wanting something too much, the battle against craving something that could ultimately destroy you in one way or another.

Love was Jasmine's personal battleground, rather than food, but she knew her war would be as long and as hard as Carmel's.

Love hurt. The more love, the more pain, and she didn't think she could bear Raziq's rejection or abandonment. The withering of his regard would stop her heart.

"Good morning." Raziq opened his eyes and smiled. Then he opened the car door and disappeared into the brush.

He strode back a minute later and opened up the back of the 4Runner. "We need to go farther off the road; the power pulsing within the earth is close." He slammed the vehicle shut and handed her a bottle of water and her small cosmetic bag that held her toothbrush and other necessities.

Putting a stripe of toothpaste on his brush, he poured water from his bottle over the brush.

Jasmine went into another stand of bushes to take care of her morning ablutions. All this uncertainty was driving her nuts. She'd almost rather dig in and fight than wander all over creation in response to vague intuition and urges.

"Do you want me to drive?" she asked, as she returned to the car.

"I'm fine," he said, starting the car. "Earth flows with water as fire flows with air. It's not that reliable, though, because some of the great lines of power run with long dry riverbeds and underground currents."

What was he talking about? Lines of power? How was that going to help them find a bottle with a genie in it? She sighed, tired of asking questions that got her answers she didn't fully understand.

Raziq handled the car deftly over the bumpy ground, avoiding hazards and holes. Jasmine allowed herself to relax. "Where are we going?"

"We're taking a shortcut to a road I found on some of my maps. I know that's the road that leads to what we're seeking."

Jasmine's heart thumped as they pulled off the gravel road into the first ghost town she'd ever seen outside of television.

"Welcome to Snake, Utah," Raziq said.

"Ominous name," Jasmine muttered.

Raziq donned his jacket and got out of the car.

"Is this where we are supposed to be?"

He nodded. "I feel it."

"The lines of power you were talking about?"

"No, the djinni." Raziq took off toward a dilapidated wooden building a little way off from the cluster of buildings in what she supposed was the center of town.

Jasmine followed him more slowly, picking her way through the brush. She stood outside the building which looked as if it were going to collapse any moment. But there was something worse, a sensation of cold dread. Something awful had happened in that building. Something awful still might happen.

She opened her mouth to call for Raziq. Then she heard him exclaim. All thoughts of her own safety forgotten, she rushed inside.

Raziq was standing in the middle of the floor.

Sunshine was pouring in through the open roof and reflecting diamond glints off the sparkling bottle he held up to the light, triumph on his face.

"Is that a genie?"

He wheeled and grabbed her and swung her in a circle. "We've done it. With the djinni's help, we'll defeat the sorceress."

"And save the world?" Jasmine added with a grin.

"Naturally. It wouldn't have been noble enough to go through all this merely to save our own skins."

"I don't mind helping the world out this once, but from now on I expect it to stay safe."

"The world is never safe. It continually requires saving. With luck, it simply won't be us required to do the rescuing next time."

He stepped back from her and started to pull the stopper from the bottle but hesitated, beads of sweat forming on his brow. Jasmine was hit with a wave of dread and nausea so strong it doubled her over.

"Do you get the feeling we shouldn't open it?" he asked.

"You think?" Jasmine said, putting a hand out against a wall to steady herself.

"Sarcasm becomes you, woman." Raziq gave a tigerish growl and she giggled. Then she yelped as the wall shifted under her hand.

Timbers rumbled and shifted. "Run!" Raziq said, grabbing her hand. Jasmine scrambled to keep up with his long legs. She panted harshly—had they come this far to have a building fall on them?

Finally, they stood a safe distance away, watching the entire side of the building collapse.

"The bottle is safe?" she asked.

He nodded. "Let's get out of here."

21

"What happened to us when you started to release the djinni?" Jasmine asked, once the spooky ghost town had receded in the distance.

"I'm not sure. Maybe my brother was trying to tell us something. I thought we were done after we had found the bottle." He shook his head. "I still have the urge to move on."

"But if we open the bottle and make the wish, can't we settle down somewhere and simply live life? Won't all this craziness be over?"

He gave a little shake of his head. "Something tells me that it's too soon. There's still something we need to do. It's not time to release the djinni. The entire universe runs on order. There's a time for everything."

"I've heard that somewhere. But when is the right time? Where are we going, Raziq?"

"South. We're going south."

Jasmine felt as if she was going to scream with frustration. Was this ever going to end? Instead, she gazed out the window, seeing nothing, thinking about the scattered pieces of her life and how she was ever going to get them to fit back together again.

Hours later, Jasmine drove through what seemed to her to be surreal dreamscapes while Raziq slept. Craggy red cliffs loomed, interspersed with ruddy canyons and rock. Scrubby bushes dotted the dusty desert under cold bright blue skies.

Raziq had stocked up on water, plenty of it. She wondered how long they were going to be out here. She shuddered. Mars seemed more homey and welcoming.

Raziq stirred and rubbed his eyes. "Why don't you pull over? I'll take over the wheel from here. We're almost there," he said.

Jasmine wanted to scream *almost where?* But she obediently pulled over and got out of the car. It didn't matter where. She'd follow this man to hell.

"Good shocks," she said, as he went off-road and they bounced over the rocky ground.

"Since I have no idea what shocks are, I'll take your word for it."

"Shocks absorb . . ." Her voice trailed away as she spied a silver ribbon cutting through the barren desert and scrub. "Do you see that?"

"That stream follows a significant line of earth power. Once a mighty river ran through here. This dying stream is all that's left."

"So we're really almost there?"

"Yes, we're almost where we're supposed to be."

Where they were supposed to be was the mouth of a red cave, cliffs protruding out of the ground like silent giants guarding either side. The silver stream ran silently past, as if it were a snake.

Raziq busied himself pitching a tent, while Jasmine cast around close by for branches to use for a fire.

Night fell and the moon rose, shining silver and bright, and a feeling of déjà vu struck her. The setting reminded her of her dream of the midnight world. She peered off into the distance.

There were the rock formations crouching like deformed demons. The stunted tree she had taken refuge within was in the distance and there was the scurry of myriad little creatures. She turned: yes, there was the cliff.

Maybe this was a sign she was where she was supposed to be, doing what she was supposed to do. After all, in the dream Raziq had saved her after demons attacked, a disquieting thought. She hurriedly gathered up the brush she'd put in the tarpaulin and rushed back to the tent.

"Are you sure we shouldn't sleep in the car? It's warded from demonic attack," she said.

"We should be out in the open, under the line of power," he answered.

Ask a simple question, get a nonanswer. But she knew that Raziq always gave her the best answer he could give at the moment. She scooped out the sand for a pit and started to lay the branches and brush for a campfire, delving into her memory for her latent Girl Scout skills. She'd cook that dehydrated vegetarian stew mix that Raziq had bought. It might be tasty, but even if it wasn't, it would be nutritious. They'd have that with tea and dried fruit for dinner.

Then they'd open the bottle, make the wish, and decide where to settle down. Yep, that was a plan.

Raziq finished unpacking the gear in the tent, and he crouched beside her. "Need help?"

"I'm doing all right. Is that stew all right for dinner?"

"Sounds fine."

The fire was blazing in no time, with the pot of stew hanging over the flames by its metal handle. She was proud of how she well was dealing with the camping stuff, especially since her idea of roughing it was staying in a Motel 6.

They sat companionably in front of the flames, leaning against each other. The flames mesmerized Jasmine. They flickered as if they were restless entities, their movements an intricate dance.

"I don't want to open the djinni's bottle tonight," he said.

She turned her head to look at him.

"Maybe the time will be right tomorrow," he said.

She stared into the flames, exhaled, and decided to let it be. His intuition hadn't led them astray yet.

Something nagged at her. "Where are those spirits, Raziq, the ones who scared the sorceress away? And why did they do that?"

"They are probably right here. They are your spirits, your protectors."

"You're telling me that I've had spirits with me my entire life?"

"I think most people do, baby."

"Then why do so many bad things happen to people? If everybody is guarded by unseen beings, they seem to do a piss-poor job a good portion of the time."

"It's the human condition to suffer, to learn, to die, to be reborn. Why would the spirits interfere with the natural order of things and the choices that other souls make?"

"Nobody would choose to watch their child die or suffer pain or starvation, but it's happening to millions as we speak," Jasmine said. "How could somebody choose to have their entire family killed?" She couldn't keep the tinge of bitterness out of her voice.

"You don't understand. Humans are spirit. They never really die. Pain doesn't last forever. The lessons lie in its reasons."

Jasmine moved a stick around in the dirt. "You're saying our lives aren't really real—that nothing we do matters."

"I'm saying the opposite, that everything you do matters. I'm saying only that human life is like a cut diamond with the sun shining through it. It's brilliant, it's beautiful, but you have to realize that this life is as if you're seeing only a few facets. To understand the true glory of the jewel, you have to pull back and see its entirety."

She nodded. "You say that I know those spirits?"

"Some choose to stick around and guide the other spirits they love through their lessons. You may have spent many lifetimes together in different guises."

Jasmine stared into the crackling flames as Raziq got up to add more wood to the fire. Her world-view shifted and broke down entirely to form something new. The problem was she didn't know quite what. She was scared and confused, running with no clear destination in sight.

"You're like a wounded animal," Raziq said.

His words jarred her. "What do you mean by that?"

"Don't bristle. I can see your aura. You've been hurt so badly in the past there are muddy gray and brown streaks. But I can see past that to the beauty of who you really are."

"What do you mean, hurt badly in the past?"

"I have no details. All I can see is your pain and its effects. I come close to comfort you, to gather you in, and you snap at me. Try to bite. But like I said, I see your pain."

Jasmine swallowed hard. She felt vulnerable and defective. She wanted to push him away, to slap him and storm into the tent. But somehow he saw her pain. How did he know her?

"When my family died, a part of me died, too," she said, her voice halting and unsure. "It was as if I had to force myself to live. I thought that feeling would go away. It never really did."

"You don't feel worthy of life. That could be it. And because of it, you've attracted people who didn't respect your worth, right?"

She looked away. "Only men," she said. "That's why—" she stopped, unable to get the words out. How could she share her deepest fear with this man who pierced through to her soul?

"That's why you won't let us love each other," he said.

Her eyes closed. His words hurt. Her deepest desire and fear were the same thing, tearing her apart.

"You can let the pain go if you choose to. Your pain and fear—they're not really you." She opened her eyes. He gazed at her, so open and kind. He reached out and touched her heart and head. "This is you," he said.

The fire cracked as if the flames were speaking to her. She stared into the flames, trying to feel all she held inside. Then the grief bubbled up, nearly choking her. But there was something else, something darker. Anger. How dare they all leave and abandon her alone to the world?

A sob escaped and Raziq handed her a tissue. She wiped her eyes.

"You've missed your calling," she said. "You obviously should be a shrink."

"Don't," he said. "Don't stuff it all back and cover it up with brittle and superficial banter. I want you to be real with me."

"Enough, Raziq." An ache was building up in her, one she rarely allowed herself to feel. "I'll try, but I can't do it all at once." She moved into his arms. "I need you to make love to me," she whispered in his ear, her body moving sinuously against his hard frame.

"Yes," he said, his breath coming out in a hiss.

22

Raziq fitted Jasmine against his hardness. He moved her gently into the tent, tumbling her down to the soft comfort of an air mattress cushioned with down-filled sleeping bags.

She removed her clothes for him with trembling fingers. His eyes absorbed her, drank her in. Every line, every curve, every dip of her body, she felt his claim.

He stood and removed his clothes far too slowly. Her eyes feasted on his masculine form, his randy arousal. She'd never tire of him, never have enough.

He moved to her and she felt his erection swell against her stomach. She wanted him lower, needed to feel him between her thighs, deep inside.

But he wouldn't rush. Tonight would be savored and sipped. They played and tasted, toying with each other, nibbling exposed skin, drinking long, lavish kisses like draughts of fine wine.

"You're mine, you know that?" he said.

She nodded, passion stealing her words. Yes, yes, yes, she was his and his alone.

"Always," she said.

Raziq cradled her body and gazed into her eyes. He kissed her again, tenderly, with a promise. Without their lips separating, he rolled her over him.

Oh yes, now. She lifted herself and impaled her body upon his stiff cock without hesitation. She moaned from the exquisite feel of his thick head entering her as the shock of it set her entire being ablaze. She was sensation: she tossed her head back and undulated her hips, rotating and teasing, making him moan and gasp, his body quivering. "Give it to me," she said.

But Raziq wouldn't give himself over that easily.

He stilled her hips with his strong hands until she barely moved at all. She felt her walls clamp around the length and breadth of him, quaking with the full pleasure he gave. Ohhh, yes. She was merciless, raising and lowering her hips again in a slow, sensual spiral, reveling in her power while he groaned in sublime agony, shuddering, sweet friction hurting so good. She advanced and retreated, urging him in a hot whisper to give it up, to surrender.

He refused to succumb. In a quick, powerful movement he took control and she was on her back. He buried his face into her neck, working downward to twirl his tongue around one stiff nipple, then the other. Then he sucked hard, sending arcs of pleasure to the core of her.

She writhed under him as he plunged in and out, hot and wet, withdrawing to the tip. She was frantic, her body on fire. She gripped her thighs around his waist tight, to capture and hold the bubble swelling inside her.

"Give it to me, baby," he whispered in her ear. "Let it go and come to me." He cupped her breasts completely, capturing her peaked nipples between his fingers, giving her all his hot thickness, rhythm tight like a drum again and again and . . . she cried out his name as the bubble reached the peak and exploded.

Her body quaked in shuddering spasms, and he was joining her ecstasy, saying her name over and over. He held her there, suspended, wouldn't let her go, turned up the heat with a deeper thrust, pulled her closer, and sealed their bodies, letting his empty completely into hers.

For several moments they lay there, locked together in the throes of aftershock, the tiny tremors continuing, their breath coming fast, dissolving together.

Then, exhausted, they slept, still connected.

Jasmine woke suddenly and looked around. Raziq slept at her side. She thought she'd heard somebody calling her name.

She dressed quickly and left the tent. Dawn rioted red and purple over the red-orange mountainous crags and canyons. Hiking to a cluster of rocks, she climbed to the top. Breathless, she gazed over the wild, rough land and felt its power throb. She raised her arms and let the energies flow to her, as she had in the astral.

Fire swept through her, pure energy. She inhaled, held it, held it, and gathered more, becoming one with the being of the world. She'd never felt more alive; it was as if she was full of life. More than she ever had been before—more real.

Power raged within her like winds whipping through her body. She raised her arms and opened her hands, streaming it to the sky. Flames rushed from her, white, orange, and blue, blazing into the dawn morning.

Jasmine was so startled that she tumbled backwards with a yell, falling from the rocks and hitting the earth with a crash.

Damn, that hurt. She lay there for a while, feeling the pulsing energies through the ground.

There was a thunder of feet and Raziq appeared. "Are you all right?" he asked, his face twisted with concern.

She tested herself. No broken bones, she was fairly sure, but she was one huge ache.

"I fell from the rocks," she said.

"What were you thinking, climbing like that? If you'd fallen wrong, you could have cracked your skull." Then he cocked his head, the thunderstorm fading from his face. "What's different?" he asked.

"I don't know. Flame shot from my hands."

"You're joking," Raziq said.

"I joke about many things. Turning into a human torch isn't one of them."

"Gods, it was you all along, not me," he said.

"What are you talking about?"

"You're the one with power. You're the one who is going to defeat the sorceress."

Raziq helped her to her feet. He was wearing only jeans and it was cold out.

"Let's get into the tent so you can dress," she said. He must be mistaken. Sorceress fighting was completely out of her ken.

* * *

"Tell me exactly what happened," Raziq said, as soon as they returned to the tent.

"I didn't do much. I went out and climbed on the rocks and fire shot from my hands."

"There was far more to it than that. Stop denying and tell me."

She sighed. "It felt as if I gathered power from the earth, the air, the entire world. The energies filled with fire and when I stretched out and willed it to release, sort of the same as moving an arm or leg, flames shot to the sky."

Raziq inhaled. "So you *are* the one with power. I never would have guessed."

"Humph. Neither would I."

"It's time for this play to begin." He drew the bottle from his jacket pocket and in a quick movement removed the stopper.

Diamond dust sparkled in the air, and a copper-skinned woman of unearthly beauty stood there clothed in what appeared to be a tawny fur cloak. "Raziq!" she cried. "I must go back—" Then the woman screamed, wavered into smoke, and streamed away. Adrianne Dimontas stood at the opening of the tent, holding out a dark glass bottle. The djinni faded to a thin stream of smoke and disappeared within it.

The sorceress stoppered the bottle triumphantly, then turned to Raziq. "What do we have here, another one?"

She produced a second bottle and pulled the stopper. She frowned. "No, not quite, it seems."

Raziq charged her.

She eluded him easily. "Silly man, what a shame and a waste." She pulled her wand from her sleeve. "You're worthless," she said as she raised it.

"No!" Jasmine screamed, feeling the power rush into her like a storm building, ready to explode.

"You," Adrianne said, swinging around. "I thought I killed you once. This time you'll stay dead."

She shifted the wand. Jasmine met the sorceress's silver wand with a wall of flame. It was a battle of wills. Jasmine pushed inch by inch toward the sorceress, feeling the woman subtly give way.

Adrianne paled, her wand outstretched, and beseeched her demons to assist her, then muttered spells in a strange tongue.

Jasmine concentrated, and power roared into her. She saw Raziq pull away from the heat, his clothing alight. He dropped, rolled, and ran.

Adrianne screamed as the flames licked closer to her skin and wheeled to run. Jasmine blocked the exit with another wall of flames, hemming her in.

Jasmine wavered as the woman screamed pitifully, pulling back the flame, reluctant to cause another human such a terrible death. But fire reveals, and in the backwash of flame, Jasmine saw faces— hundreds, thousands, an uncountable number expressing agony, grief, and death. She witnessed the suffering Adrianne had caused, and worse, the evil and anguish the sorceress would accomplish in the demons' names if Jasmine wasn't strong enough to finish it completely, here and now.

Jasmine let the flames sweep over the woman. The screams stopped. Jasmine pulled the fires back to her, and a still-flaming blackened bundle fell to the ground, giving off the sickening odor of burned flesh.

Jasmine staggered past the corpse, lurched outside, then fell to her knees and retched.

Raziq tangled his fingers in her hair. "You did it," he said, his voice touched with wonder. "You saved the world, girl."

23

Raziq watched as a strange wind rose and whirled all that was left of Adrianne Dimontas, gray ash, into the air and away. The sorceress was gone, body and soul. Nothing was left except a dark bottle.

Raziq straightened and retrieved the djinni's bottle. He pulled the stopper out, hearing Jasmine's simultaneous cry of protest.

Yoni appeared out of a puff of smoke and smiled at him. "Thanks, bro," she said.

He lifted an eyebrow. "You've been watching too much television."

"It's the addiction of the remaining remnant of our people," she agreed.

"Where should we leave her bottle, Raziq? Here?" Jasmine asked, approaching.

"Don't be rude. Jasmine this is Yoni, an old, old acquaintance."

Yoni considered her. "She reminds me of Hyeth," she said.

"She's completely different. Hyeth was docile, biddable and content."

"Hyeth was content enough, but she was in awe of you, unlike this woman. You were one of the few great djinn left in the world. She banked her fires for you."

Raziq frowned, not wanting to return to the aching, dim memories of millennia ago.

"This woman is so like Hyeth, she could share her soul," Yoni said.

"Please stop discussing me as if I'm not present," Jasmine snapped.

Raziq suppressed a grin. He bet Jasmine had almost busted something trying to keep her mouth shut during the last minute or so.

Yoni bowed to her. "I apologize. I was out of line. I was only struck by your resemblance to a former acquaintance."

"Is that true? Raziq, do I look like your ex-wife?"

"You look nothing like Hyeth. And if you did, what would it matter? She's returned to the earth, with no part of her remaining."

"I meant an inner resemblance," Yoni added. She turned to Raziq. "I see you've gained a great appreciation for being human."

He nodded. "I knew they continued, but I couldn't get past the concept of death. But now—now it's not bad at all."

"Humans inherited the earth. Partly spirit, they continue, unlike us, bound to the flesh." Yoni looked sad. Then she brightened. "What is your wish, Raziq?"

He stared at the sky, then glanced over at Jasmine, who seemed to be fascinated with her footwear all of a sudden. "I want her to see her mother again," he said. Jasmine's head snapped up. He repeated it twice more.

Yoni smiled. "You've wished for something I can give." The air sparkled. An unbearably bright light appeared in front of Jasmine. What appeared to be a door opened, and a dark woman appeared, small in stature and slim with her smile wide and beaming.

Jasmine sank to her knees, overcome with emotion. "Mom!" she cried.

Justine Flynn rushed to her daughter and pulled her up into her arms. "It's wonderful to feel you again," she said.

Jasmine trembled, unable to speak.

Her mother cupped her face and looked deep in her eyes. "I'm not here to stay." She drew Jasmine to her feet. "Walk with me, child."

Jasmine's fingers intertwined with her mother's. She felt her mother's warmth by her side, smelled her familiar, never-forgotten scent. "Why can't you stay?" she asked, her face wet with tears.

"Because I'm dead, baby." Justine halted at an outcropping. They sat with their backs against the rocks. Jasmine leaned against her mother in a position she remembered from childhood, feeling cradled and comforted despite her mother's inarguable words. Mom was dead, and there was no denying that reality. Except for the fact that right now, Mom was here.

"I'm sorry you had to suffer so," her mother said.

"I wasn't the one who died!"

"But we didn't suffer. Your brother and father moved on long ago. I've stayed close to you. I know how much you've needed me."

Jasmine lifted her head. "You're one of the guardian spirits Raziq speaks of?"

"Yes. I've done what I can."

"You saved my life in that hotel room," Jasmine said.

"My finest hour. You should have seen the look on the witch's face."

Jasmine laughed, then sobered, remembering all the hot sex. "And Raziq, you've seen—?"

"People do what people do. Nobody is that different, honey, and there's nothing to hide about the human condition. But I have seen how much he loves you—and how much you deny it."

"I love him too, Mom."

"I didn't say you deny your love for him: you deny his love for you." She stroked her daughter's hair. "Your pain was so great, I thought it would kill you, but you made it. It scarred you though, scarred you down deep."

Jasmine felt something release within her. "I wish I could have died with you! Why didn't I? It's not fair, Mom."

"Things are as they should be. Everything you've experienced makes you the person you are. You've been refined by fire. You're the one who's supposed to be in this world now, not me, not your father or your brother."

"But I'm not a good person. If you only knew . . ."

"I know everything you've done. You forget I've been by your side all these years. You felt unworthy, and offered yourself to men who didn't value you, who had other women. Since you've always been the other woman, you reap the karma of your actions. But you've repented and paid for your errors. It's time to move forward."

"What do you mean?"

"I'm speaking of your insecurity over your man, and your fear of losing him to another woman. Let it go. He loves you." Her mother met her gaze. "You love your friend, Carmel. Would you allow another to replace her in your heart? Could another replace me? Love is faithful and sure. As long as you have his love, you should have no fear."

"What if he stops loving me?"

"You are his choice. You fascinate and stimulate him. You're his soulmate. Why would he? People change less than you think. It's just as likely that you might stop loving him. But that is as impossible as the sun not rising tomorrow, hmmm?"

A weight lifted from Jasmine's chest. She felt light, as if she could fly. "Thank you, Mom. You mean so much to me."

"I know, honey. But you need to let me go." Justine looked weary all of a sudden. "I just want to go home."

Jasmine sobered. "What's it like to be dead? I've always wanted to ask somebody that," she added.

Justine grinned. "Not as bad as most people believe. But I've been here, with you, so I don't rightly know all the mysteries. But something pulls me higher. It feels as if I've been too long away from home."

Tears stung Jasmine's eyes and she embraced her mother fiercely. "I love you so much. Go, go now."

"I love you too, baby. You always were my heart and always will be. I'm leaving you now, but you'll be all right. Take care of that man because he's going to take care of you. Take care of my grand-babies, too."

Her mother looked off to the distance, a look of pure joy transforming her features. The she tenderly kissed her. "We'll be together again, baby," she said, and slowly became one with the light, blazing more intensely than the sun through and around Jasmine.

Jasmine leaned her head against the rock and wished her beloved mother a blissful trip back home.

Jasmine walked back to Raziq alone, lighter than she ever remembered feeling, her burden lifted, and her grief finally released. He was breaking camp, packing up, getting ready to move on.

She walked up behind him and he spun around as he heard her approach and straightened.

She walked straight into his arms. "Thank—"

He touched her lips, cutting off further words. "I wanted to give you at least a portion of your wish to have your family back. I know it wasn't enough—"

"It was more than enough." Emotion welled up within her. "It meant everything to me—to see my mother, and now she's free, gone on home." She looked into his dear face. "I can never repay you."

"Yes, you can," he said.

"Anything," she answered without a second's hesitation.

"Marry me, have my children."

Something cracked within her soul and every defense, every wall she had left came crashing down. She opened up to this man, this wonderful man, and handed him her heart. "I love you, Raziq Djinn, and there is nothing I want to do more."

He kissed her, his lips both tender and hungry. "I love you," he said when he lifted his head. "And I can't imagine existing without you by my side."

Jasmine looked into this wonderful man's eyes, the other half of her soul, and for the first time in her life, she no longer felt alone. "You won't have to," she said.

"Let's go," he said.

"Where?" she asked.

"Home. Let's go home," he said.

She nodded. "I'm ready."

Epilogue

Months later, Jasmine sat on Bless's wide porch swinging back and forth on a cushioned swing. The sun was setting on an unseasonably warm afternoon. She sipped lemonade, content to her bones, watching her husband pull through the gate.

Raziq walked up the porch steps and Jasmine tried to struggle to her feet; her belly was swollen, heavy with child.

"Don't get up, baby," he said as he sank down beside her. He kissed her, then rubbed his face in her hair. "You always smell so good," he said.

"How did it go with the house?" she asked.

"Signed, sealed, and delivered." He patted a sheaf of papers in his jacket pocket.

They'd closed the deal on their new home a couple of hours away. They'd live closer to Atlanta than Bless and Rick's place, but still in the country, on five acres of land, lush with pine and wildlife.

"How's he doing?" Raziq asked, caressing her stomach.

"Practicing for his soccer tryouts," she said. She settled against Raziq.

He picked up her hand, fondling the huge pink diamond he'd given her at their wedding. "Mine?" he asked, his voice barely audible. Her heart swelled as she heard volumes of Raziq's love and need in that one word.

"Always," she answered, filling the word to overflowing with the love she held inside for him, for the family they were starting. Sometimes she wondered if she were big enough to hold all her happiness inside. It seemed to spill out and overflow, her joy contagious.

He helped her to her feet, and they walked together into the blazing light of their future, hand-in-hand.

Dear Reader:

I've wanted to write Jasmine Flynn's story since late 1999 when she appeared in *The Look of Love* as the sassy, man-loving best friend of Carmel Matthews.

This book is different from my paranormal romance *In My Dreams*, but it has the same basic premise. The final apocalyptic battle between man and demon is coming. But some gifted humans, the Chosen Ones, are prophesied to eventually defeat the demons and save the race of man. The demons are determined to eliminate this threat while the Chosen are helpless infants—and it's up to their parents to protect them. *In My Dreams* and *Love's Potion* both feature one of these special couples who are each charged with protecting one of the Chosen Ones.

Magic and love seem to go together naturally. I hope you love reading this book as much as I enjoyed writing it.

Wishing you love and magic always,

Monica Jackson

Check Out These Other
Dafina Novels

Sister Got Game
0-7582-0856-1

by Leslie Esdaile
  $6.99US/**$9.99**CAN

Say Yes
0-7582-0853-7

by Donna Hill
  $6.99US/**$9.99**CAN

In My Dreams
0-7582-0868-5

by Monica Jackson
  $6.99US/**$9.99**CAN

True Lies
0-7582-0027-7

by Margaret Johnson-Hodge
  $6.99US/**$9.99**CAN

Testimony
0-7582-0637-2

by Felicia Mason
  $6.99US/**$9.99**CAN

Emotions
0-7582-0636-4

by Timmothy McCann
  $6.99US/**$9.99**CAN

The Upper Room
0-7582-0889-8

by Mary Monroe
  $6.99US/**$9.99**CAN

Got A Man
0-7582-0242-3

by Daaimah S. Poole
  $6.99US/**$8.99**CAN

Available Wherever Books Are Sold!

Check out our website at www.kensingtonbooks.com.

Look For These Other
Dafina Novels

Grab These Other
Dafina Novels
(mass market editions)

Grab These Other
Dafina Novels
(trade paperback editions)

Every Bitter Thing Sweet
1-57566-851-3

by Roslyn Carrington
$14.00US/$19.00CAN

When Twilight Comes
0-7582-0009-9

by Gwynne Forster
$15.00US/$21.00CAN

Some Sunday
0-7582-0003-X

by Margaret Johnson-Hodge
$15.00US/$21.00CAN

Testimony
0-7582-0063-3

by Felicia Mason
$15.00US/$21.00CAN

Forever
1-57566-759-2

by Timmothy B. McCann
$15.00US/$21.00CAN

God Don't Like Ugly
1-57566-607-3

by Mary Monroe
$15.00US/$20.00CAN

Gonna Lay Down My Burdens
0-7582-0001-3

by Mary Monroe
$15.00US/$21.00CAN

The Upper Room
0-7582-0023-4

by Mary Monroe
$15.00US/$21.00CAN

Soulmates Dissipate
0-7582-0006-4

by Mary B. Morrison
$15.00US/$21.00CAN

Got a Man
0-7582-0240-7

by Daaimah S. Poole
$15.00US/$21.00CAN

Casting the First Stone
1-57566-633-2

by Kimberla Lawson Roby
$14.00US/$18.00CAN

It's a Thin Line
1-57566-744-4

by Kimberla Lawson Roby
$15.00US/$21.00CAN

Available Wherever Books Are Sold!

Visit our website at www.kensingtonbooks.com

Grab These Other
Thought Provoking Books

Adam by Adam
0-7582-0195-8

by Adam Clayton Powell, Jr.
$15.00US/$21.00CAN

African American Firsts
0-7582-0243-1

by Joan Potter
$15.00US/$21.00CAN

African-American Pride
0-8065-2498-7

by Lakisha Martin
$15.95US/$21.95CAN

The African-American Soldier
0-8065-2049-3

by Michael Lee Lanning
$16.95US/$24.95CAN

African Proverbs and Wisdom
0-7582-0298-9

by Julia Stewart
$12.00US/$17.00CAN

Al on America
0-7582-0351-9

by Rev. Al Sharpton
with Karen Hunter
$16.00US/$23.00CAN

Available Wherever Books Are Sold!

Visit our website at **www.kensingtonbooks.com**